'Who are you

'No one at the m

Charlotte stared a

William grinned and propped his hip on the table, disturbingly close to her. 'I thought you were getting straight to the point,' he teased, and it dawned on her that he had deliberately misread her question.

'Don't be silly,' she mumbled, and she heard a low chuckle.

Dear Reader

We look at special care baby units with Josie Metcalfe's
SECRETS TO KEEP, Caroline Anderson returns
to the obstetrics unit—more babies—at the Audley
Memorial in ANYONE CAN DREAM, while each
heroine has a secret to keep from the hero. You
will *love* William and Jacob! We welcome back
Sharon Wirdnam with CASUALTY OF PASSION,
Meredith Webber's UNRULY HEART repatriates ill
people, and both books bring couples back together.
A good month's reading!

The Editor

Caroline Anderson's nursing career was brought to an
abrupt halt by a back injury, but her interest in medical
things led her to work first as a medical secretary, and
then, after completing her teacher training, as a lec-
turer in Medical Office Practice to trainee medical
secretaries. In addition to writing, she also runs her
own business from her home in rural Suffolk, where
she lives with her husband, two daughters, mother and
assorted animals.

Recent titles by the same author:

ONCE MORE WITH FEELING
NOTHING LEFT TO GIVE
ROLE PLAY
A MAN OF HONOUR

ANYONE CAN DREAM

BY
CAROLINE ANDERSON

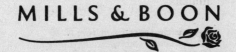

MILLS & BOON

MILLS & BOON LIMITED
ETON HOUSE, 18-24 PARADISE ROAD
RICHMOND, SURREY TW9 1SR

*First published in Great Britain 1994
by Mills & Boon Limited*

© Caroline Anderson 1994

*Australian copyright 1994   Philippine copyright 1995
This edition 1995*

ISBN 0 263 78969 1

*Set in Times 10 on 11½ pt. by
Rowland Phototypesetting Limited
Bury St Edmunds, Suffolk*

03-9502-44424

Made and printed in Great Britain

CHAPTER ONE

HE WAS all man.

From the soft, gleaming strands of his almost black hair, down past the frankly assessing, clear blue eyes, over the stubborn chin, the very male throat, the cluster of dark curls that crowded the V of his theatre pyjamas, down again, past the broad shoulders and deep chest, the lean hips propped negligently against the table, over long, strong legs to the big white anti-static boots that clad his feet, he was completely, entirely, unequivocally a man.

He threw back his head and laughed at something the ward sister said, and Charlotte swallowed. That laugh, rich, deep, full of enjoyment—this was clearly a man who reached out and seized what life had to offer.

She just hoped to God he didn't think she was on the menu, because he was also a work colleague, and as the senior registrar, probably more her boss than the consultant would be. They would work closely together—sometimes very closely, she thought, and a moan rose in her throat, threatening to suffocate her.

No! her mind screamed. Why not a woman? Or a wimp? Or one of those safely married, charming but very non-threatening men that the department was lousy with?

Why him? And why her, for God's sake? What had she done to deserve it?

He tipped back his head and drained the cup in his

hand, and she watched, riveted, as that masculine throat worked.

He dropped the paper cup in the bin and turned to the ward sister, saying something to her.

Charlotte missed the words, hearing only the voice—deep, mellow, like bitter chocolate, it seemed to melt inside her, swirling into the deepest recesses of her subconscious, calling to something long-buried and detrimental to her peace of mind.

The ward sister turned towards her and said something, but she couldn't focus on it. All her senses were in confusion, her whole psyche thrown into chaos by his voice.

She heard the voice again, but this time, she realised, addressing her.

'Earth calling Charlotte—come in, please.'

She looked up—straight into that mesmerising blue gaze. She swallowed again. 'Mr Parry—I'm sorry, I was miles away.'

A smile—slow, teasing, too damned understanding—touched his lips, lending them a sensuous curve. 'I noticed. I hope this isn't an omen, Dr Jennings?'

'Omen?' she croaked.

'Yes—a portent of things to come.' He shrugged lazily away from the table, growing even taller. 'I hope,' he said slowly as he approached her, 'that your concentration is usually a little sharper?'

'Um—much.' She came to an abrupt halt, backed up against the door-frame.

'Good. I'm going round the ward in ten minutes, when I've got out of this fancy dress. You've just got time to acquaint yourself with the notes. Oh, and by the way. . .'

'Yes?' The word sounded strangled.

'Call me William.'

She drew in a breath as he squeezed past her in the doorway.

The breath lodged, then eased out slowly in a deep, anguished sigh as he strode out of sight. He hadn't touched her—not quite—and yet every nerve-ending had been alerted to his nearness. Though why she should feel anything—and how she could, after all that had happened—escaped her fuddled senses.

'I should stir your stumps,' the ward sister told her, cutting through her reverie at a stroke, and pushed the notes trolley towards her. 'He's got the patience of a saint with the mums, but with the medical staff he can be a bit of a tartar. You're looking for the notes with the blue tabs.'

And she left her to it. Rapidly, feeling the imminent press of time and not wishing to be on the wrong side of such an overwhelmingly powerful personality, Charlotte dived into the notes. She was still reading when there was a firm, light tread in the corridor and a shadow darkened the door.

'OK?'

'Um—yes. Who are you seeing?'

'No one at the moment. How about you?'

She stared at him blankly. 'What?'

He grinned and propped his hip on the table, disturbingly close to her.

'I thought you were getting straight to the point,' he teased, and it dawned on her that he had deliberately misread her question.

Hot colour chased up her cheeks, and she ducked her head so that her dark hair slid round her face and concealed her embarrassment.

'Don't be silly,' she mumbled, and she heard a low chuckle.

'Ah, Charlotte, don't spoil my fun. It's been a lousy weekend—aren't I even allowed to tease you a little? How about a smile—just a tiny one, for me?'

She was over-reacting, of course. She knew that, but some sorts of conditioning went so deep they were difficult to set aside. Still, try as she might the smile refused to come.

'I'm sorry,' she said quietly. 'My social skills are a little rusty.'

His face was still smiling, but his eyes were searching, piercing, analysing.

She felt naked inside, and she looked away awkwardly. 'Which patients are you seeing this morning?' she tried again.

'Ah. Well, let's see all of them, shall we? Have you had time to skim through the notes?'

'Only briefly. I wouldn't like to have to make any decisions or judgements based on what I've had time to read,' she said hastily.

'Don't worry,' he assured her. 'I wouldn't expect you to in your first few days. This morning is all obstetrics—a couple of postnatal checks after the weekend, three mums going home who need an OK for discharge, and an antenatal—a woman we're inducing. I want to see how she's getting on. Then at ten we've got a short theatre list—two elective Caesarian sections and a cervical suture to remove. Then lunch, a quick flit round the gynae ward and a clinic this afternoon, then back to the ward to check the section mums and have a cuddle with the babies.'

She glanced up at him in surprise. 'A cuddle?'

His grin was slow and lazy. 'Oh, I always try and find time for a cuddle.'

Her pulse unaccountably thumped, and her eyes were drawn to the strong, long-fingered hands that lay linked in his lap. What would it feel like to be cradled by those hands?

Safe.

Her eyes pricked with tears, and she turned away, dropping the notes back into the trolley.

'Sounds like a busy day. Perhaps we'd better get started.'

It was busy—hectic, even. Her knowledge of obstetrics was scant and almost all theoretical. When William told her to reach into the opened uterus at the second Caesarian section and lift out the tiny, slippery infant, she thought for sure she would drop it.

The midwife standing by quickly took over, lifting the baby over the drapes and showing him to his delighted mother and father before cleaning him up and clamping the cord after William had removed the placenta. His father then held the baby while William checked the uterus for any fragments and closed up, swiftly and efficiently.

Through it all Charlotte stood rooted to the spot, her eyes fixed on the wall opposite, and when they wheeled the woman out and went to change she walked into the staff lounge in the theatre suite and dropped into a chair, still stunned.

That baby had felt so—oh, dear God, so tiny, so fragile, so *precious* in her hands——

'You'll learn more, faster, if you watch me instead of the clock,' a dry voice said from just above her.

She glanced up. He looked serious, angry even, for some reason. She looked away.

'The clock?' she said blankly.

'Yes—the clock. You were watching it as if you expected it to explode or drop off the wall or something.'

'I didn't even see a clock,' she told him. 'It was just. . .'

She felt his anger recede, and he dropped to his haunches in front of her. 'Was it the operation itself? Did you feel queasy?'

She shook her head. 'No, it was. . .' She struggled to explain her confused feelings. 'I've never taken part in a delivery before. It's the first time in my life that my hands have been the first to touch another human being. It just—hit me.'

She looked up, meeting those shatteringly blue eyes, and was relieved to see his expression gentle as understanding dawned. His hand covered hers, hard and strong and warm—safe, as she had expected. His voice softened.

'It's wonderful, isn't it? Your first baby—rather like your first kiss, or the first time you fall in love. No other delivery will be quite so special—the first time you do a straightforward vaginal delivery on your own without me around to take over and interfere will be pretty special, too.'

'But that very first touch will never happen again,' she said softly, and his fingers tightened, squeezing her hand in recognition of her tumbled emotions.

'No. No delivery will ever be quite so significant again.' He stood up. 'OK, we've got a suture to remove now—a woman with an incompetent cervix who habitually aborts at four months. We've managed to keep her going this time, and she's really excited.'

'When will she go into labour?'

He laughed. 'Probably before she leaves the theatre. She's had the odd twinge in the last few days, so although she's still not due for a fortnight we thought we'd take it out. It's not her first full-term delivery— they've got a boy of seven—so her pelvic floor won't hold her up for long, I don't suppose!'

They scrubbed again, gowned up and went back into the operating-room. The lady was just being wheeled through the doors, her face slightly apprehensive. She smiled when she saw William, and he walked over to her and stood beside her head.

'OK, Penny?'

'Bit nervous.'

'Don't be. It may be a little uncomfortable—just do your breathing exercises and think of the baby.'

'Oh, don't,' she said with a shaky laugh. 'I hardly dare.'

'What? Silly girl, you'll be fine, and so will the babe.'

'I wonder what it is?' she said thoughtfully. 'I've tried so hard not to think about it, just in case. . .'

'Well, let's get the suture out and you'll soon know the answer, won't you?'

The nursing staff positioned the woman in the lithotomy stirrups, and then William sat himself down between her legs and held out his hand.

The scrub nurse passed him a speculum liberally smeared with gynacological jelly.

'This might be a bit chilly,' he warned the patient, and then deftly inserted it and opened the jaws.

'Here, Charlotte, can you see the end of the suture?'

She could, just about, by bending down and putting her head right beside his. She felt the slight scrape of his stubble against her cheek, and forced herself to concentrate. At the top of the vagina, right up where the cervix passed through the vaginal wall, she could just make out a little tail of thick silk.

'It looks fairly inaccessible.'

'Long instruments,' he told her, then added with a chuckle, 'Getting it out's the easy bit. Getting them in there is much more of a challenge!'

The scrub nurse handed him a pair of forceps. He located them on the free end of the suture and tugged, then, using a pair of special scissors, he wriggled one blade under the knot.

'Ooo, that hurts,' the patient said tentatively.

'Sorry. Just try and relax, Penny, we're nearly there.' He closed the handles of the scissors, and Charlotte saw the cervix slowly blossom as he drew out the thick piece of silk. 'That's it, all done.' He checked the cervix again, then withrew the speculum and stood up. 'OK?'

She smiled shakily. 'Is that it?'

'Yup. You can go and have your baby now, but give us time for a quick cup of coffee, eh?'

She didn't. From the moment the suture was released her cervix was dilating rapidly, and when Charlotte and William went back down to the ward twenty minutes later they heard the squalling cry of a new baby coming from the delivery-room.

'She can't have done it that quickly,' Charlotte said in amazement.

'Unless we've had another admission during the time we were in theatre, she has,' William said, and stuck his head round the delivery-room door.

'Penny?'

'Oh, Mr Parry—she's a girl. Come and see!'

Charlotte followed him in, to see a tiny, delicate

little baby cradled against the woman's bare breast. Tears were streaming down her cheeks, and her husband beside her was fighting with his emotions.

Charlotte didn't bother.

'She's gorgeous,' she said, her voice choked. 'Well done.'

William looked startled for a second, then grinned.

'Well, well, well,' he said softly, and Charlotte felt like kicking him. Why shouldn't she share their happiness?

She watched as he stared down at the baby and smiled, and then ruffled the woman's hair gently. 'Clever girl,' he murmured. 'How are you feeling?'

'Wonderful.'

Her husband looked stunned. 'We never thought we'd make it,' he said, still choked. 'But she's here, alive and well—thanks to you.'

William grinned self-consciously. 'We aim to please,' he told them.

After a few more moments of admiration and praise, he opened the door for Charlotte and followed her out into the corridor.

'Don't say a thing,' she warned, scrubbing the tears from her cheeks, and he laughed, his breath soft and warm against her neck.

'Would I?'

'I don't know. Very probably.'

He chuckled. 'Rumbled. Oh, well. How about some lunch and then we've got this clinic to do?'

They had just settled down to their lunch when his bleep squawked.

'Oh, hell,' he muttered, and, cramming a mouthful in, he stood up and crossed the room in a few quick strides. There was a phone on the wall and he picked it up, dialled the switchboard and spoke.

Charlotte watched him, fascinated by the play of emotions across his face, the way the light from the window highlighted the breadth of his shoulders and the straight, square set of his legs, feet planted firmly on the floor.

He was a very attractive man, and by his own admission seeing no one at the moment. A few years ago, Charlotte would have picked up on his interest, the mild flirting, the odd teasing remark, and she might have seen where it would lead them.

Now she felt oddly threatened by his attraction to her, and even more so by her attraction to him. That was much more dangerous.

Still, it was only a matter of degree and there was nothing that could persuade her to get involved with him, no matter how attractive.

Once bitten, and all that.

He was coming back towards her now, waving at someone and greeting them with a laughing remark.

Her heart twisted. What would it be like, she wondered, to be so universally popular? Everyone she had seen that morning had seemed to like him, from the ward sister through the theatre staff to every patient they had come across.

Now she saw him with his colleagues, pausing to exchange a quick word with Alex Carter, head of another obs and gynae firm. Charlotte had seen Alex about the hospital and always thought he looked rather severe, but he didn't look severe now, laughing at something William had said.

He rejoined her then, sliding into his seat and tossing her a grin. 'Patient we started inducing last night with a prostaglandin pessary is getting close. When we've eaten we'll go and have a quick gander at her, and then we can go and start the gynae clinic. OK?'

She hoped so. Surely he wouldn't leave her either with the delivery or the gynae clinic—not on her first day in the department?

'Do you expect any problems?' she asked.

'No. Straightforward delivery, hopefully, but she's had a few problems in her pregnancy and we've been watching her closely.'

Charlotte's heart sank. 'Problems?'

He waved a fork. 'Nothing drastic, just a bit of a blood-pressure hike. She'll be fine.'

Charlotte hoped so. She didn't fancy doing her first delivery on a patient with pre-eclamptic toxaemia!

She finished her modest meal and watched as William hastily swallowed the last of his huge portion of chicken tikka, gulped down a cup of coffee and picked up the sticky bun off the tray.

'I'll eat this as we walk,' he told her, and tore a chunk off it with large, even teeth.

Good grief, he was so physical, she thought helplessly as she followed him back, struggling to keep up with his long, easy stride. His feet ate up the corridors as surely as those gleaming white teeth disposed of the bun, and almost as rapidly.

By the time they arrived at the lift that would take them to the ward, he had finished the bun and she was breathing hard.

'Are you unfit?' he asked her, watching her chest rise and fall with interest.

'No—my legs are shorter than yours,' she retorted, and he tipped his head on one side and pretended to study them.

'So they are—but somewhat more elegant. Pretty ankles.'

She blushed, and he grinned and ushered her into the open lift. The doors slid shut, and she was suddenly aware of the close confines and the overwhelming presence of this big and very attractive man.

She turned away, making a pretence of looking in the mirror and tucking an escaping strand of glossy brown hair back behind her ear. She would have to take it down and put it all up again before the clinic.

She felt him watching her, and as she glanced up in the mirror her violet-blue eyes met his bright corn-flower gaze and locked; for a long moment he said nothing, then the lift slowed and the doors opened to admit a gaggle of laughing nurses.

'Hello, William,' they chorused, and he grinned at them.

'Hello, ladies. All well?'

He chatted easily to them as they went up to the ward, and Charlotte felt the tension in her ease. Then the doors swished open and with an impersonal hand that felt like a branding iron he ushered her out of the lift.

His hand fell away naturally as they cleared the door, but Charlotte could feel its imprint in the small of her back for what seemed like hours. Her heart sinking, she realised that he was a toucher, one of those people who didn't shy away from physical contact but touched and patted and hugged as easily as most people breathed.

For Charlotte, who found all but the most necessary physical contact almost threatening, working with him would be difficult in the extreme. Once again she wondered how on earth she was going to cope.

*   *   *

The woman didn't require any assistance from them for her delivery, but William was called to repair the tear in her perineum after the gynae clinic, and he turned it into a lesson for Charlotte.

Somewhat shy herself, she wondered how the woman would cope with having two of them discussing such an intimate area of her body, but William laughed and chatted and smiled at her over the drapes, and talked constantly about the baby while he worked, so there was no possibility of any shyness or inhibition.

He was so natural, such an easy communicator, and Charlotte found herself relaxing as she watched over his shoulder.

'Can you see the different muscle layers underneath?' he asked her at one point, and she had to steady herself against his shoulders as she leaned forward. She could feel the bones of his shoulder beneath her hand, and the solid column of his spine against her body.

'I think so. Which groups are they?' she asked him, and was annoyed that her voice was a trifle breathless.

He pointed out the various muscles by name, and then showed her where the muscle fibres had separated. 'See—there's a little tear here. You have to be careful not to miss that sort of thing or you can leave the patient susceptible to a prolapse of the posterior wall of the vagina—and we don't want that, do we, Karen?'

'Certainly not,' the patient replied with a laugh, and Charlotte watched as he drew the torn muscle layers together with soluble sutures.

'There. The skin is the easy bit, but because the area is so well-supplied with nerves you don't want too many knots, and you have to be careful not to put them in too tight or when the tissues swell they hurt like the dickens, don't they?'

'I couldn't sit down for weeks with the first,' Karen agreed.

'Ah, well, you had a large episiotomy, if I remember rightly from our previous conversation.'

'That's right—he was a breech.'

'How old is he now?' William asked conversationally as he put in a subcutaneous running suture.

As they chatted, Charlotte watched with interest and not a little trepidation. Would she be able to repeat this procedure with his guidance? Because one thing was certain—he wasn't going to be able to spoon-feed her forever.

Within a very short time the suturing was finished and William slid back the stool and rolled his head on his neck, standing up and stretching.

'All done,' he told the patient, and stripped off his gloves. 'Now, I need a cuddle with this baby— if I may?'

The woman laughed. 'Be my guest—actually, I wouldn't mind a cuddle with him myself.'

'I'll bring him to you,' William promised. He washed his hands, dried them and went over to where the nurse was just finishing the baby's bath.

'Hello, little chap,' he said softly. 'May I?'

The nurse nodded, and Charlotte watched, fascinated, as William's big hands slid round under the baby and lifted him confidently into the crook of his arm.

As the baby's cheek brushed against the fabric of William's white coat, he turned towards the big man, his tiny mouth open, searching.

'He's rooting—here, I think he wants to be fed.'

The midwife propped the woman up into a sitting position, and then William perched on the bed and passed the baby to his mother.

'Hello, my darling,' she crooned softly, and, lifting her gown, she settled the baby expertly at her breast.

In seconds the room was filled with the rhythmic sucking sound, and they left the happy pair alone to their blissful feed. As they walked back up the ward together, William glanced at the clock on the wall.

'Just after six. Not bad, for a day that was supposed to end at five.'

'When did it start?' she asked him.

He laughed. 'Oh, two this morning—and yesterday finished just before midnight.' He paused at the door.

'Fancy a drink?'

She shook her head. 'No, thanks—I've got a pounding headache.'

'Maybe another time,' he said, and, turning away, he thrust the door out of his way with the flat of his hand and strode quickly towards the lift. 'I'll see you tomorrow,' he threw over his shoulder.

She watched him go thoughtfully. She hadn't lied. She did have the most frightful headache, but there was more to her refusal than that.

She made her way home, weary, her mind full of the new things she had seen and done—her first delivery of sorts, the gynae clinic, the happy mothers with their babies—and William, of course, larger than life, full of warmth and compassion, his skilled hands steady, strong and yet gentle.

She regretted not going for a drink with him. It might have been fun, and one quick drink wasn't going to affect their relationship.

Still, it was too late now, and probably just as well. She took some pills for her headache, but it was joined by another ache, deep in her heart, that nothing could ever take away.

CHAPTER TWO

THAT first week was fascinating for Charlotte. Despite the August heat that made everything close and muggy, the windows in the tall maternity block were open and it was light and airy, a pleasant place to be.

She found herself shadowing William constantly, always at his elbow being instructed in one technique or another, and when on Thursday night he finally allowed her to do the night on call he insisted on being around just in case.

'Anything at all, you call me. You can clerk the patients on admission, and you can handle any of the slightly tricky deliveries, but I want to be there beside you. OK?'

She nodded, not feeling in the least that she was being mollycoddled unnecessarily, because she had discovered that in obstetrics things could happen very fast, and when they did the window for correcting the problems could be frighteningly small.

One woman was admitted in labour shortly after William disappeared off down the corridor leaving her in charge. She clerked her, then checked with the midwife that all was going well, and went for supper, then went back up to the gynae ward to check that there were no problems requiring her attention.

She was bleeped while she was in the gynae ward and went back to the maternity ward to find that a woman was asking for sleeping pills. She wrote her up for some, then checked on the patient in labour again.

'I think it's going to be quite slow, but that's fine,' the midwife told her. 'When she's a little further on she wants to use the water pool, so if you'd like to observe I'm sure she won't mind.'

Charlotte was fascinated. Delivery-wise it had been a slow week, and she was itching to see the water pool and other equipment in the birthing centres in use. So far the only deliveries had been in the normal delivery-room, but she gathered from talking to the nursing staff that that was unusual.

Certainly the trend now was towards more natural labours, and the hospital was extremely well-equipped to supply the needs of the informed new mothers.

Now all she needed was a little practical experience!

She went into the ward office and wrote up some notes, and then later on was called up to gynae to write up some pain relief for a post-op case.

At four o'clock, when she was feeling distinctly drowsy, the midwife found her at the central work station sipping a black coffee.

'Things are hotting up,' she told Charlotte. 'She's had a rest, and woken to stronger contractions, so I've got the pool filling and I'm going to pop her in it in a few minutes. Want to come and see?'

'Is that OK with her? I don't want her to feel threatened by my presence—you know, as if it's necessary to have a doctor there.'

The midwife, Sue Coulter, shook her head. 'It's OK. I've told her you're doing your GP training and that you're just interested, and she and her partner are quite happy with that.'

So Charlotte finished her coffee and went into the birthing centre, in time to see Sue slipping off the woman's gown and helping her into the large, deep pool.

Like a high-sided paddling-pool, it was about six feet in diameter and two feet deep, so that the woman could float in the warm water. Moving was easier, and the lapping of the water around her distended abdomen was very soothing. Her partner was bare-chested, and as the woman lay with her head on the side of the pool and her legs drifting in the water he reached round her and stroked the swollen curve with gentle, circular movements.

'Oh, that's wonderful, Mick,' she said softly.

'What's the smell?' Charlotte asked Sue.

'Aromatherapy oils—lavender and jasmine oil mainly, but possibly some others.'

Just then the woman started moaning rhythmically, her voice rising to a crescendo and then dying slowly away as the contraction eased.

Charlotte thought it sounded as though she was in a great deal of pain, but Sue explained that she was just releasing the power of her body.

'It often sounds worse than it is. Many of the women who deliver conventionally in silence actually suffer far more because it's all internalised and they don't release the tension. You can see Jet is actually very relaxed.'

Charlotte could see that; she could also see the support and love her partner was giving her, the tender way he held her, the soft murmur of his voice in her ear, the tiny little kisses against her cheek.

Another contraction followed, then another.

'They seem to be coming thick and fast,' Charlotte commented to Sue.

'They often do—the water seems to accelerate

labour at the same time as it eases the pain—incredible, really, especially for women who want to avoid pain relief.'

Just then Jet had another contraction, and Sue listened to the baby's heart with a waterproof Sonicaid.

'Lovely—it's doing really well,' she announced.

'I want to float face down but I'll drown,' Jet said after the waves had passed.

'No problem,' Sue told her. 'Have you ever used a snorkel?'

She nodded. 'Yes—I used to swim a lot.'

Sue handed her a bright yellow snorkel tube, and, fitting it in her mouth, Jet turned over on to her front and floated, arms and legs bent slightly, drifting in the warm water. When the next contraction came she pulled herself to the side, her legs spreading automatically, and, lifting her head out of the water, she began to moan again.

Three times she did that, and the fourth she turned over, her expression totally focused as she began to grunt.

Sue quickly reached down into the water and examined her by touch alone, and then smiled.

'Nearly there, Jet. Keep going, my love, just one more gentle push—lovely, stop now and pant—that's it—little pants—good girl—that's it—and again—lovely!'

Jet cried out, her face a mixture of pain and relief, and, reaching down, she stroked her baby's head in wonder.

'Are you sure it can't drown?' she asked, showing the first sign of concern, but Sue shook her head.

'Oh, no—the chest is still compressed. Once the body's delivered that's different, so we lift them up quickly then, but now no, it's perfectly safe.'

Jet sighed gently and leant back against Mick's arms. 'Oh, here we go,' she groaned, and with a long, deep grunt she pushed and Sue lifted the tiny baby clear of the water and placed it in the woman's waiting arms.

'Oh, Mick, look,' she said, tears mingling with the water on her face, and her partner reached round and cradled his child, his own tears flowing just as freely.

'What is it?' Sue asked.

Jet bent her head and looked more closely, then lifted a face dazed with happiness. 'She's a girl.'

'Congratulations,' Sue said warmly, and Charlotte couldn't help the little bubble of happiness that rose up inside her.

The pain, she knew, would come later, but for now the beauty of the moment carried her willingly along.

After a few minutes, when the cord had stopped pulsating, Sue severed it and handed the little girl to Charlotte. 'Here, you have a cuddle while Mick and I help Jet out of the water and dry her off a bit.'

The child was tiny—minute, delicate little fingers that gripped Charlotte's own and wouldn't let go, her eyes clear and bright, fixed on Charlotte's face.

The ache in her heart seemed to grow until she could almost feel the swelling in her chest. What would it be like, she wondered, to hold your baby in your arms? To have that serious gaze trained so intently on your face, and know that you were the most important person in that tiny child's world?

All too soon Jet was warm and comfortable on the bed with the baby settled again at her breast, then with a minimum of fuss she delivered the placenta, exclaiming over it in fascination.

'I never saw it with the first one,' she told Sue. 'Isn't it amazing?'

Sue lifted up the membranes and showed how they had enclosed the baby, and Jet reached out a hand and touched the fine tissues.

'It seems incredible that they can be so strong,' she said in wonder. 'They're so thin. I thought they'd be thicker, tougher, somehow.'

Her gaze dropped back to the baby. 'She's lovely.'

Charlotte smiled. 'She is—very beautiful. Well done.' Her arms felt achingly empty. She turned to Sue. 'Any needlework for me to do?'

Sue was busily tidying up at the business end, and paused thoughtfully.

'Little graze on the back wall—it should be OK. The perineum's intact and there's no muscle damage.'

Charlotte, who hadn't yet handled a repair alone, was only too relieved. She thanked the couple for allowing her to witness the birth of their baby, then went back out into the ward.

It seemed hectic after the tranquil scene she had just witnessed, a bustling, chaotic mass of busy people all going about their endless tasks.

Ants, she thought, bustling, busy little ants. And what for? Perhaps because everyone else's arms feel empty, too.

As she walked towards the nursing station to find out if anyone was looking for her, she saw William striding towards her. His eyes met hers, and a quick smile touched his eyes.

'Hi. How's it been?'

'Fairly quiet,' she told him. 'I've just witnessed my first water birth.'

'Ah—peace and tranquillity?'

'Oh, yes—it was beautiful. Actually, I wanted to talk to you about it when you've got time, because I've heard all sorts of things about it being dangerous, but it seemed incredibly un-dangerous, somehow.'

He nodded. 'It all boils down to screening and vigilance. Have you had breakfast?'

She shook her head.

'Let's go down to the canteen, then, and we can talk while you eat. I could do with another cup of tea.'

When they were settled at the table, Charlotte tucking into her steaming pile of bacon and egg and tomato, William with a cup of coffee and a similar plateful with an additional stack of toast—'Looks too good to walk past,' he'd said—they turned back to the subject of water births.

'So,' he asked, lazily stretching himself out sideways and propping one elbow on the table, 'what do you want to know? The history?'

She shook her head. 'I know the history of water birth, from Moscow in the 1960s to Leboyer and Odent, and now thanks to them and people like Janet Balaskas and the Active Birth Centre it's used extensively in this country, particularly for home births. Right?'

He nodded. 'Right. You've done your research.'

'I should hope so,' she retorted. 'Still, books can only tell you so much. It's the other things.'

'Like?'

'How long have you used water pools here?'

'Oh, about a year. The old boy thinks they're akin to witchcraft, but Alex Carter and his team are firmly in favour.'

Charlotte assumed that 'the old boy' was Derek Blythe, the consultant in charge of their firm, who was known for being firmly rooted in the interventionist era. He had a higher rate of Caesarian sections, forceps deliveries and episiotomies than any of the other consultants, and she had already discovered that the midwives regarded him as a hazard to be avoided at all cost! It followed, therefore, that if he was against water births, then the midwives were very likely to be for them.

William confirmed her thoughts. 'I have yet to speak to a midwife who disagrees with it provided it's used only when appropriate,' he told her.

'Which is?' Charlotte asked.

'Oh—we tend to rule out multiple pregnancies, malpresentations, previous adverse history, anyone who needs monitoring electronically—and of course the midwife has the authority to get the mother out at any time if she feels things aren't going well.'

'How often does that happen?'

He shrugged. 'Not often. When necessary. People tend to want to get out of the water themselves if they lose confidence for any reason, or want to feel more securely screwed to the floor—the loss of gravity is a bit unsettling for some, but nearly everyone finds the time they spend in the water helps them enormously.'

Charlotte nodded. 'Jet seemed to cope very well.'

'Jet? Oh, damn, I missed it!' he said, clearly disappointed. 'Oh, well, how did it go?'

'Lovely.' Charlotte told him all about the birth, and he nodded in satisfaction.

'Good. Great. She had a fairly grim labour with the first, apparently, and we were hoping this would be better for her. We've noticed a huge decrease in the amount of pethidine we've used since we've had the pools—we put the second one in only a couple of months ago because the first had been so successful. Now there's hardly a day goes by when they aren't in use, and it seems to make an enormous difference to the level of pain women feel.'

He tore off a chunk of toast and eyed Charlotte speculatively. 'Are you doing anything tomorrow night?'

The change of subject fazed her.

'Tomorrow?' she said blankly, casting about for a more feasible excuse than washing her hair.

'Mmm. Only I've got a Janet Balaskas video and a whole lot of articles on the subject—I thought you could come over and look at it and talk it through with me.'

Peversely, disappointment warred with her relief. Only business after all, she thought, and then gave a little sigh.

'That would be fine. I haven't got any other plans.'

'Great. I'll give you the address—have you got anything to write on?'

She fished in her handbag and came up with an old envelope.

'Do fine,' he said, and she watched as he scribbled the address in a broad, bold hand, then drew a little map on the bottom of the scrap of paper. 'OK?'

She took it, noticing again his long, straight fingers and the way the dark hair sprang away from the skin all around his wrist, in sharp contrast to the blinding white of his coat. Strange how something so ordinary could be so absolutely fascinating, she thought absently as she tucked the envelope back in her bag.

'About seven?'

She nodded. 'That would be fine.'

'Good.' His smile warmed her, but his next words

chilled her right back down again. 'Don't bother to eat,' he said. 'I'll knock something up during the evening—make a change from eating alone.'

She nearly protested, but something in the quality of his voice stopped her. Instead she met his eyes, and beneath the gentle smile she saw a lonely man. So she didn't refuse, because she too had spent too many Saturday nights alone with nothing but the telly for company. One less couldn't be a bad thing.

It was a tall, red-brick Victorian semi in a quiet residential road close to the park. Quelling her misgivings, she parked outside under a glorious copper beech tree and walked briskly up the red and black diamonds of the front path to the door.

There was a bell-pull set in the wall, the brass gleaming, and as she tugged it she heard a bell jangling far inside the house.

She saw him through the leaded lights, walking swiftly up the hall, and the door swung inwards to reveal him dressed in impossibly sexy jeans and a loose, startlingly white silk shirt. The cuffs were rolled back to reveal a tantalising glimpse of those sexy forearms, and Charlotte's breath caught.

'Come in—you're right on time; my directions can't be that bad.' He gestured for her to come in, and his lips curved in that ready smile she found she was beginning to look for more and more.

She returned the smile and handed him a box of after-dinner mints. 'Here—my contribution to the meal. I'm afraid I know nothing about wine, so I thought it was safest!'

He took the box with a smile. 'Perfect,' he said. 'I don't drink anyway, but these will really hit the spot.

Come on through—I thought we'd go in the conservatory and take advantage of the last of the evening sun.'

She followed him down the long hall, past several doors and through a bright, airy kitchen with white units and a tiled floor, out into a very traditional Victorian-type conservatory.

He gestured to a wicker chair with fat, squashy cushions on it, and she perched on the edge and looked down the garden.

'Oh, how pretty!'

'It's lovely, isn't it? It was a mess when I moved in, but my mother's a landscape gardener and she designed it for me.'

He handed her a tall glass, clinking with ice and beaded with condensation. 'Here—you look hot.'

'I am—it's been a scorcher,' she agreed.

He lowered himself on the other chair and stretched out luxuriously with a sigh. 'Oh, it's nice to sit down.'

'Have you been working?' she asked in surprise.

His grin was wry. 'Only on the house—it was a tip. Still, it needed doing!'

Charlotte squirmed guiltily. 'You shouldn't have done that—not for me.'

He laughed. 'You didn't see it! Anyway, it had to be done before Monday. I have a Mrs Mop, but she's gone off to Majorca for a holiday and left me to my own devices for a week. If she came back and saw it like it was, she'd give me the sack.'

She smiled, as she was meant to, and sipped the cool, refreshing drink. 'Oh, this is lovely.'

'Is it OK? It's an alcohol-free spritzer, because I knew you'd be driving.'

'It's perfect.' She rolled the ice-cold glass against her forehead. 'Mmm.'

He stood up abruptly. 'We're having a salad,' he told her, his back towards her. 'All sorts of bits of this and that. OK?'

'It sounds delicious,' she told him, puzzled by his sudden exit from the conservatory. 'Anything I can do?'

'Talk to me while I make the vinaigrette.'

She had slipped off her shoes, and padded silently over the cool tiles into the kitchen.

'What about?'

He jumped and turned. 'Damn it, woman, don't sneak around—you'll give me heart failure!'

She giggled. 'Sorry.'

A slow grin crept across his face, and he lifted his hand and brushed his knuckles across her cheek.

'I'll forgive you—as you're so lovely.'

Charlotte swallowed, suddenly feeling trapped.

'Don't be silly,' she said, but her voice sounded thready and slightly strangled.

'I wasn't.' For once his voice was serious, and she felt his hand again, open this time, his palm dry and cool against her flushed cheek. His thumb stroked softly under her eye, then round, grazing her bottom lip. It caught, tugging gently, and she felt desire shoot through her.

'William,' she pleaded, but whether for him to stop or go on she didn't know.

However he stopped, and she was shocked at the wave of disappointment she felt. He turned away, his jaw working, and started pouring ingredients into a little bottle. 'Do you mind raw garlic in the dressing?' he asked, and she heard a slight rasp in his voice.

So it wasn't just her.

'No—no, that's fine,' she told him a little blankly,

her eyes mesmerised by the jumping muscle at the corner of his jaw, just in front of his ear.

He bent and took something out of the fridge, and her eyes followed his movements, savouring the taut pull of the jeans over his neat bottom, the glimpse of dark hair on his chest through the buttons of his shirt as he turned back, the flexing of muscle in his forearm as he pressed the fresh garlic and scraped it into the bottle.

He lifted his eyes, spearing her with a brilliant blue gaze. 'If you watch me like that, you're likely to land yourself in deep trouble,' he advised gently, and she swallowed.

'I'm sorry.'

'Don't apologise—I was enjoying it.'

Her eyes fell, and she swallowed again. Was it her imagination, or did his jeans fit more snugly than before? She looked hastily away. This was ridiculous. She had never intended this to happen when she came here tonight! She must be out of her mind, ogling him and giving him ideas. Women like her——

'Penny for them.'

She shook her head, and then started as his hands closed over her shoulders and turned her back towards him.

'Let's get this out of the way, shall we? Then perhaps we can both concentrate.'

Oh, God, he's going to kiss me, she thought in desperation, and then it was too late to think, because those sensuous, beautiful lips were on hers, like the touch of a butterfly, light and delicate, searching.

She made a tiny *moue* of sound and his arms slid round behind her, coaxing her up against his long, rangy body as his mouth settled more firmly against hers. She felt the warm tip of his tongue caress her lips, and her mouth opened of its own accord to receive his kiss.

His tongué felt like velvet, warm, coaxing, seeking hers out and dallying with it, then retreating, encouraging hers to follow in a little dance.

She played along, fascinated by the texture of his mouth, the clean, sharp edge of his teeth, the firm fullness of his lips—and his taste, sweet and fresh, with a faint trace of mint.

He eased away, sucking her lower lip into his mouth and nipping it gently with his teeth. The sharp stab of desire shocked her and she jerked away, her eyes wide, her chest rising and falling with her ragged breathing. Their eyes were locked, and she was stunned at the raw animal need etched on his face.

He quickly blanked it and moved away.

'There—that wasn't so bad, was it?' he said casually, but his voice was as ragged as her breathing and his body betrayed him.

She felt her shoulders droop. What happened next? Was she expected to sleep with him? Sing for her supper, so to speak?

Her silence must have registered, because he put down the bowl of salad he was carrying and came over to her, his hands cupping her shoulders and kneading gently.

'Charlotte, it's all right. We don't have to take this anywhere if you don't want to.'

But I do! she wanted to shout, but couldn't. Anyway, if they did he would soon lose interest in her.

Funny how much the idea of that hurt.

She shook her head helplessly. 'I thought we were looking at a video.'

'We will—hell, Charlotte, I wasn't trying to get you here under false pretences. I don't work like that. If you want to watch the video, we'll watch the video. If you want to talk, we'll talk. If you change your mind about——' His broad shoulders shifted in a little shrug, and his mouth tipped slightly. 'Let's take it hour by hour, shall we?'

'Can we?' she asked, doubtful.

'Oh, yes. Let's start with supper because I'm starving, then we'll go and watch the video and look through the literature, and then—well, we'll see.'

'No,' she said, her panic surfacing finally through the haze of desire. 'No, we'll have supper and watch the video, and then I'll go home. I don't care if you accuse me of running away——'

'Charlotte.' His voice was softly reproachful. 'I'm not going to accuse you of anything, and you certainly don't need to run anywhere. You can walk away from me at any time.'

She didn't believe him. Experience, she had found, was the best teacher, and when it came to escape she was very experienced.

Except usually she had had the sense to do it long before this point.

Only once before had she failed to escape, and she had paid the price for years. In many ways she was still paying it, and probably always would.

She backed away.

'I—I need a drink,' she said feebly, and, turning swiftly, she almost ran back into the conservatory.

He didn't follow her, but left her, curled up on the chair among the squashy cushions, facing firmly down the garden, her thoughts in turmoil. Her body was still throbbing, aching with a need she hadn't known she could feel, and she clutched the cold glass like a lifeline.

After a few minutes she heard him come up behind her and touch her gently on the shoulder.

'Charlotte?'

She stiffened. 'Yes?'

'Supper's ready. I thought we could eat it out here, if you like.'

She closed her eyes. 'Supper?'

'Come on.'

He helped her up, holding her when the pins and needles stabbed her feet where she had sat on them, and with an understanding smile he led her to the table in the kitchen. The food was spread out—cold meats, dressed salads, a huge bowl of frilly lettuce, chunks of crusty brown bread, a big block of pale yellow butter —and she stared at it blankly.

'Charlotte, what is it?' he asked softly.

She looked up at him, at the blue eyes searching her face, the broad, strong brow furrowed slightly in concern, the mouth, so gentle and yet so powerful, the instrument of her downfall.

'It's you,' she said bluntly.

'I'm not a threat.'

'Yes, you are—to me.'

He shook his head. 'No. It's something else. Something old that's still hurting you.'

Hurting? Yes, she supposed it was. 'I'm divorced,' she blurted out.

'And?' he coaxed.

Her shoulders twitched in a little shrug. 'He was a pig. I find it difficult to relate to men.'

'Did he knock you about?'

She laughed, the sound high and strained. 'He didn't

need to. There's more than one form of abuse.'

He said nothing, but his eyes spoke volumes. Reaching for her, he turned her silently into his arms and enfolded her in a wordless hug of comfort.

'Poor, poor girl,' he said finally, and his hand smoothed over her hair, as if she were a hurt child. She felt his lips press against her head, the gentle gesture strangely soothing, and her arms slid round his sides and hung on.

He felt so good—big, safe, like a rock in the crazy world of her see-sawing emotions.

He held her like that for ages, till she was calm again —although not perfectly calm, because underneath she could still feel that raw, untamed need simmering gently, just waiting for another excuse to leap into life.

She gently disentangled herself from his arms, and turned away.

'Here.'

She found a pristine handkerchief in her fingers, and was amazed to realise she had been crying.

'I'm sorry,' she whispered.

'Don't be. You've got nothing to be sorry for. Come on, let's eat and go and watch this film, then if you like we can talk about it.'

'It?'

'Yes, it. Whatever it is that's eating you up inside.'

Strangely the thought of talking to him didn't frighten her any more. It would almost be a relief to share the nightmare at last—or part of it. Some—the worst bit—was hers and hers alone.

That she would never share.

The meal was delicious, and the video of three water births was fascinating, although she cut herself off deliberately from the emotion. They watched it twice, talking through it the second time, and then he turned off the television and handed her a file.

'All sorts of bits and pieces—press cuttings, extracts from journals—have a browse while I make the coffee.'

She did, finding the research information fascinating, and when William came back into the room she was totally engrossed. She read to the end, then set the file down and looked up to find him watching her, a curious expression on his face.

He patted the sofa beside him. 'Come and sit here and drink your coffee, and tell me all about yourself.'

She laughed awkwardly. 'All?'

He grinned. 'Well, some, then.'

'Can't I stay here?'

'No.'

'Why?'

'Because I can't kiss you when you're sitting there.'

She stood up, her heart thumping, and walked across the dimly lit room.

'Here.'

He turned sideways so that one leg was against the back of the sofa and pulled her gently into the V of his thighs, so that her back was cradled against his chest and his arms rested lightly across her waist.

'Now—tell me all about this rat who hurt you so badly.'

'Greg?'

'Was that his name?'

She nodded. 'He was OK at first, I suppose. I was very naïve—an only child, and my mother died when I was young. I didn't think there was anything odd about waiting on him hand and foot—it was something

I'd always done for my father, and it seemed natural to carry on.'

'But?'

She shrugged. 'He never seemed to appreciate anything. At least my father had been grateful for my efforts in the house, but Greg criticised everything I did. The cooking, the cleaning, the ironing, even——'

'Yes?'

She ran out of courage. 'Nothing.'

He sighed, a soft puff of breath that teased the hair on the back of her neck and sent shivers down her spine.

'Don't tell me—the bastard called you frigid.'

She stiffened, the word still jabbing through her like a knife.

'Oh, Charlotte. . .' His hands slid up her arms, coming to rest on her shoulders. 'Poor, poor baby,' he murmured, and she felt his thumbs working deeply in the muscles of her neck, soothing, easing the tension. She dropped her head forward and let him touch her, then gradually the touch changed, growing less soothing, more sensuous. He turned her in his arms, so that her side rested against his chest, and one hand tipped her chin up so that she was facing him.

'I'm going to kiss you,' he said softly, and then his head came down and his lips settled against hers.

The desire was back, sharp and shocking as before, but this time she was helpless to pull away. Instead she reached for him, winding her arms around his neck and tunnelling her fingers through the soft, thick hair at his nape. She felt a hand, warm and strong but gentle, cup her breast, and she arched against it, a little cry rising in her throat. His fingers were against her skin somehow, inside the blouse, under her bra, working the sensitive nub of her nipple to an aching peak.

His mouth left hers, trailing hot, steamy kisses over her neck and throat, down over the slight swell of her breast to close over the tender bud of flesh. She cried out, clutching his head and holding it close, and he made a guttural sound of satisfaction, switching his attention to the other aching breast that was clamouring for his attention.

Her breath was sobbing now, the sensation so exquisite that she was almost beyond reason.

'William,' she moaned, reaching for him, and he turned so that she was under him, stretched full-length on the sofa, his legs locked with hers as his mouth returned to claim her lips again.

She arched against him, her body now beyond her control. In the distance she could hear her voice pleading, but the words were meaningless. Her blouse was open now, and she tugged at his shirt, ripping the buttons in her haste.

'Steady,' he laughed, but his voice wasn't steady, and nor were his hands as he wrenched off the shirt and came back to lie against her, the soft, slightly wiry hair on his chest chafing against her unbearably sensitive nipples.

'Please,' she begged, and seconds later she felt his hand slide between them, easing her skirt aside and cupping the aching mound of her womanhood in his hard, hot palm.

She bucked under his hand, needing more, needing him, but he was in no hurry now, his fingers making slow, leisurely explorations of their own.

She felt his hand slip under the edge of her tiny bikini pants and move down again, the long, strong fingers probing, searching for something.

He found it, his touch unerring, and Charlotte felt something inside her give and shatter.

'William,' she sobbed, and then the sensations flooded her, blinding her, leaving her shaken and weeping in his arms.

'Frigid my aunt Fanny,' he said softly, and, smoothing her skirt down over her trembling thighs, he gathered her in his arms and held her till she was quiet.

Then he lifted his head and stared down into her face. 'Your eyes are like crushed pansies,' he murmured.

'More like crushed tomatoes,' she said with a sniff.

He chuckled. 'No. You look gorgeous.'

She felt hot colour flood her cheeks. 'I feel an idiot,' she told him candidly.

'Why?'

'Why? I just—after what I did—why?'

He laughed again, his voice softly teasing, and hugged her. 'You were beautiful. Warm, soft, all woman.'

Something occurred to her.

'What about you?' she asked shyly, dreading his reply.

'What about me? I'll live.'

'But you. . .'

'I said I'll live,' he repeated, but she could feel the hard ridge against her thigh and knew he was still aroused.

She wished she felt confident enough to return the compliment, but the whole experience had left her shaken and she didn't feel she could cope with any more.

It seemed she didn't have to. He eased his weight

off her and retrieved his shirt, gazing ruefully at the ripped buttonholes.

'Oh, well,' he said philosophically, and tugged it on anyway. Charlotte sat up, acutely aware of her bare breasts, and struggled with the catch on the back of her bra.

'Let me,' he offered, kneeling down at her feet, and, reaching round her, he clipped the catch together easily.

'You've done that before,' she said, struggling for a teasing note, and he grinned like quicksilver.

'Once or twice.'

He drew the edges of her blouse together and buttoned it, his fingers steady now, and as she looked down at his bent head a huge well of some nameless emotion rose up inside her.

'William?' she said tentatively.

He lifted his head. 'Yes?'

'Thank you.'

For a second he was silent, then his arms came round her and crushed her against his chest. 'My pleasure,' he murmured.

'I rather thought it was mine,' she said with a sniff.

'Don't be pedantic.' He winked and got to his feet. 'Coffee?'

She nodded. 'Please. I'll help you.'

She followed him out to the kitchen and looked around. There was a litter of plates and dishes all over the worktops, and she moved quickly to the sink and started running the water.

Instantly his hand reached round and turned off the tap.

'Leave it,' he said. 'I'll do it in the morning.'

'Oh, no, it's the least I can do.'

A blaze of anger flared behind his eyes, and he laid his hand over hers on the tap, preventing her from turning it on again.

'No. You don't have to earn favours in this house, Charlotte.'

She flushed. 'But I can't just leave it all——'

'Yes, you can, and you will.'

'But——'

'No more buts. Come on, the coffee's done. Let's go back into the sitting-room.'

She followed him with a sigh. If only he'd let her tidy up, then she needn't feel so guilty about——

'Stop it.'

'Stop what?'

'Trying to balance the books. You've had fun, so you have to pay—is that right? Is that what he did to you? If you went out and enjoyed yourself, you had to pay for it?'

She flushed, and he reached for her and pulled her down on to the sofa against his side.

'Oh, Charlotte,' he said softly.

She straightened away from him. 'I'm all right,' she said.

'In a pig's eye.'

'I am—really.'

'Is that why you're on your own? Because you're all right?'

She looked at him blankly. 'You're on your own, too. If everything's so hunky-dory in your world, how come you haven't got a nice cosy little wife and family?'

Something shifted in his face, some lingering regret.

'I never said everything was hunky-dory in my world,' he said quietly.

'Are you divorced too?' she asked him, and found herself dreading his reply.

He shook his head. 'No—not divorced. My wife's dead. She died five years ago.'

CHAPTER THREE

IN THE next few days, Charlotte ran that conversation through her head over and over again, but the shock of it didn't leave her. Instead she found herself growing more and more curious about the circumstances of his wife's death.

He had said nothing more, changing the subject and leaving Charlotte with the distinct impression that it was a topic that was strictly taboo.

She hadn't stayed long after that, driving home to her flat and going straight to bed, to lie there and remember the warmth of his mouth, the touch of his hands, and the incredible sensations he had wrought in her.

That he had denied himself still amazed her, all these days later, and the other thing that amazed her was how easy it was to work with him in the hospital without shame or embarrassment. She had expected at the very least to feel uneasy, but he was his usual warm, open self, and any fears she'd had were soon laid to rest. In fact he was so busy putting her at her ease that she ended up wondering if the whole event had been completely meaningless for him.

On Wednesday night they were on duty again, and, although Charlotte by this time had had a little more experience and had even done her first unsupervised repair, still William insisted on being close at hand.

'It wouldn't take you long to come from home,' she reasoned, but he wouldn't be moved.

'If you don't recognise a problem quickly enough, that extra five minutes could make all the difference. Mrs Rimmer doesn't seem to be getting on all that fast, and I'd rather be around.'

So she agreed, and in the end she was glad because in the early hours of the morning one of the midwives, Bev Linari, was about to get the switchboard to page Charlotte just as she arrived back on the ward after a coffee break.

'Oh, you're back. It's Mrs Rimmer—she's making no progress. I've had to get her out of the water and I think the baby's becoming distressed—we need to use the ventouse.'

This special vacuum cup which was applied to the baby's head and used rather like forceps had almost taken the place of the more brutal tongs of previous years, especially since the advent of silicone cups, but so far Charlotte had used neither, and said so.

'Is William about?' Bev asked.

'Yes.'

The woman's face cleared. 'Good—you know his nickname, do you? Dr Ventouse?'

Charlotte smiled. 'Really?'

'Oh, yes. He's fantastic. Get them to call him and come in, could you?'

'Sure.' Charlotte turned back to the desk and used the phone to ask the switchboard to page William, then followed Bev into the delivery suite.

The woman, Mrs Rimmer, was looking very tired and despondent, and Charlotte understood from Bev that she had requested no pain relief in the interests of the baby.

Now, however, she was getting more and more

distressed, probably with worry, and Bev and Mr Rimmer were busy calming her down.

Just when Charlotte was convinced she was going to have to learn about the ventouse by trial and error, William walked in, took one look at Mrs Rimmer's face and took charge.

After examining both the progress chart and the patient, he explained that the baby wasn't descending fast enough and was beginning to get rather tired.

'Like you, really,' he said with a grin, and Mrs Rimmer smiled weakly back.

'What I want to do is help the baby down, using your contractions to do the work and the vacuum cup to guide the baby's head in the right direction, because what's happening is it's turning slightly and getting jammed. Now, I know you don't want any pain relief like pethidine, but how would you feel about local anaesthetic?'

'Is it necessary?'

He shrugged. 'I don't know. I hope not, and I'll be as gentle as I can, but it may not be very pleasant. One thing I can assure you is that it will hurt a lot less than forceps, and it may even be better than a normal unaided delivery. It's just getting the cup on that can be a bit tricky.'

Tricky wasn't the word for it, Charlotte thought a few minutes later as William tried yet again to position the silicone cup against the baby's undescended head.

Finally he was satisfied that it was correctly positioned, and, having tested it with a low vacuum, he turned up the wall suction unit to maximum and used Mrs Rimmer's contractions and a slight twist of his wrist to correct the baby's position. Then the baby's progress was visibly improved, and within a couple of contractions William had lifted the head up and out, using the fingers of his other hand to guard the perineum.

Charlotte was amazed. Not only had the woman had very little pain from the placing of the cup, she hadn't torn on delivery of the head and was going to suffer no side-effects at all from the instrumental intervention.

'You must teach me how to do that,' she said in an aside to William once they were sure the baby was all right.

'No way,' he told her laughingly. 'It's my party trick—anyway, your fingers are too short.'

The Rimmers were delighted with their little son, and Bev was beaming happily and thoroughly enjoying the moment.

'How about a nice cup of tea?' William asked Charlotte, and she agreed readily.

They went out into the ward kitchen and William reached for the kettle, filling it and switching it on. Then he leant back against the worktop, folded his arms and grinned.

'So, how's it going? Will we make an obstetrician of you yet?'

She laughed. 'I shouldn't think so. Frankly the whole business terrifies me. I mean, they come in healthy and with very set ideas and high expectations, and then something goes wrong and whoosh! All their confidence vanishes, the delivery turns into an obstetric nightmare and you come galloping in like the cavalry. Yee-hah! Dr Ventouse to the rescue!'

William chuckled. 'Oh, Charlotte, you exaggerate. Anyway, most of the time nothing happens at all.'

'Humph!'

'Humph yourself. What are you doing on Friday night?'

'Sleeping,' she said without thinking.

'Interesting—want some company?'

She blushed. 'Why do you ask?'

His grin was cheeky and suggestive. 'I should have thought it was obvious.'

The blush deepened. 'About Friday,' she said patiently. 'Why did you ask about Friday?'

'Oh. There's a barbecue in the grounds in aid of our SCBU and the Cystic Fibrosis Research Trust—Jack and Kathleen Lawrence are organising it. I wondered if you'd like to go.'

A barbecue, she thought. A bit of harmless fun in the open air with plenty of other people around them. That should be safe enough.

'Thank you, that would be lovely,' she replied, and spent the next two days wondering if it would be harmless fun, or if it would simply be an exercise in frustration.

The most frustrating thing, she decided on Friday evening, was finding something to wear. It was so long since she'd had any kind of casual social life that she wasn't sure what was expected of her. She almost rang her sister, but the ensuing Spanish Inquisition would have been intolerable, so she chickened out and opted instead for glaring at her meagre wardrobe.

It wasn't helpful. Nothing jumped off the rail into her arms, and in the end she settled on some pretty floral cotton trousers, flat shoes and a floaty silk blouse that dressed the whole thing up a bit.

Her hair she twisted up into a clip, and then as an

afterthought she put on a dash of warpaint to hide behind.

Anything else? she thought, and her eye caught a little bottle of perfume her sister had sent her for Christmas. She still hadn't even tried it, but now, tugging off the top, she puffed it lightly on to her throat and arms.

Then it hit her.

'Oh, no,' she moaned, and ran to wash it off, just as the bell rang. 'Oh, no!' she said again, but it was too late.

She opened the door and stepped back. 'Come in, I have to wash,' she told him bluntly.

His face was puzzled. 'Why?'

'I stink—this perfume. . .'

He breathed deeply, and his eyes widened slightly. 'It's wonderful,' he said softly. 'Warm and musky.'

'I smell like a polecat.'

He chuckled. 'No, you don't. You smell gorgeous.'

'Liar.'

'I'm not. Trust me, I like it.'

'Well, I don't. I'm going to wash.'

She did her best, but it was in her hair and on her blouse, and all she managed to do was dilute the effect.

She went back to William, lounging comfortably on her settee, flicking through a magazine.

'Happy now?' he asked with a grin.

'Not really, but I've got rid of what I can. I don't know what possessed me.'

'Who gave it to you?' he asked.

'My sister Linda. Why?'

He moved closer, his eyes glittering. 'Because I want to thank her.'

She backed away. 'Shall we go?'

He grinned. 'Certainly. Are you taking a jumper in case it gets cool later?'

She thought it was unlikely to, judging by the look in his eyes, and vowed to kill Linda at their next meeting. However, she picked up a cotton cardigan the same pansy-blue as her eyes, and followed him out to the car.

She was relieved, now she had time to notice, that he was wearing jeans too, but this time with a denim shirt. He looked younger, very sexy and devastatingly handsome. Charlotte wondered not for the first time what on earth he saw in her.

An easy conquest, she thought, still ashamed of her ready response to him less than a week ago. She hoped desperately that he didn't think the musky perfume was a deliberate come-on.

They arrived at the hospital and found the barbecue just getting under way.

Ross Hamilton had been volunteered as one of the cooks, and was busy flipping burgers and stirring sliced onions on a griddle. 'Roll up, roll up,' he called out. 'Burgers, bangers, buns—roll up, roll up!'

William grinned at him and asked for two hot dogs with onions, then asked how his wife was getting on.

'Oh, bigger by the minute. Baby's not due till October, but I reckon it'll be quite large.'

'Probably just a great long streak like you,' William teased, and Ross grinned uneasily.

'I hope so. She had trouble with the first—Alex is going to scan her and if it looks tight at thirty-eight weeks he'll either induce her then or go for a section. I know which I'd rather.'

'The section?'

'You guessed!' Ross said with a laugh. 'I suppose

it's because I'm a surgeon, but it just seems more orderly, somehow!'

'You worry too much,' William told him. 'She'll be fine. Second babies are always easier.'

'Hmm.' He turned his attention back to the sausages, and William shook his head and looked down at Charlotte.

'Ketchup?' he asked.

'Please.'

He squirted a liberal dollop down her sausage, and the bottle splurted and dripped on her hand.

'Allow me,' he said huskily, and, lifting her hand, he licked the sauce off with his tongue.

The sharp stab of desire that plunged through her took her breath away, and she yanked her hand back. When she looked up again, he was observing her with interest, a predatory smile teasing his eyes.

She must be mad to be here with him, she thought bleakly. Quite mad. She inched away from him.

However, he wasn't about to let her ignore him that easily. Throwing a casual arm around her shoulders, he tugged her into his side and led her over to a noisy group. 'Let's go and join in the laughs,' he said, his hand firm and dry, burning through the thin fabric of her blouse.

She tried to ignore the jut of his lean hip, the way he paced himself to her stride so that their hips and thighs moved together in harmony. Instead she forced herself to concentrate on the group they were approaching, to see if she could identify any of them. Some were familiar—Alex Carter, one of the other obstetric consultants, and his wife Jo; Jake Hunter, Alex's SR, with his pregnant wife Annie; Andrew Barrett, one of the paediatricians regularly in evidence on the maternity wards, with his wife Jennifer, also pregnant—— God, she thought, are they all pregnant?

Charlotte knew that Lizzi Hamilton, hovering near Ross at the barbecue, was also pregnant, and there was a woman with her who was in what had to be very late pregnancy, whom Charlotte thought she recognised as Bron Henderson.

Four, she thought, and that's just the ones that show!

Their arrival in the little group was greeted with enthusiasm and some discreet speculation. William was clearly a regular and accepted member of the group but she felt their reaction to her was perhaps slightly guarded.

Had they all known his wife? Surely not, because she had died five years before and Charlotte knew William had only been at the hospital for two years.

So was it just her imagination?

She decided after a while that it was, that her natural shyness had led her to believe she was unwelcome, because the others were kindness itself to her.

She didn't talk much, but found herself watching William. As usual he stole the show, with his big laugh and expansive gestures and warm enthusiasm. He ought to sell double glazing, she thought—he'd be a natural!

Then he turned and caught her eye, and under the laughing exterior she saw a simmering need.

There was a band playing near the fence, at the limit of the hospital grounds, and he tipped his head towards it with a slow, lazy smile.

'Fancy a dance?'

'On the grass?' she stalled.

'There's a raised dance-floor, but I had in mind a

more private dance under the trees,' he said softly.

Charlotte's heart thumped. 'All right,' she agreed, but her knees felt weak with anticipation. The night was closing in now, the velvet sky clear and star-studded—a night for lovers, she thought.

They reached the shelter of the trees and William turned and drew her gently into his arms, locking his fingers over the small of her back and easing her up against him.

'Ah, Charlotte, you feel good,' he sighed, and, resting his cheek against her hair, he swayed slowly against her.

How long they stayed like that she didn't know, but nor did she care. It just felt so absolutely, completely right to be in his arms, his body warm and firm under her hands, his head bent close. No words were necessary, and when he lifted his head she made a small sound of protest.

'Come home with me,' he said.

There was no pressure, no effort to coerce, no overt attempt at seduction. She felt he was deliberately keeping his suggestion low-key so that she couldn't accuse him later of seducing her.

It was pointless, though, because he only had to breathe and she was aware of it. Everything he had done, every movement he had made had fuelled her imagination and tormented her body.

The previous week had only served to whet her appetite. Now she needed more, needed him, needed to be what she had never been—a woman, loved and wanted for herself.

And if she was only fooling herself that he loved her? Did it matter? Would it hurt anyone? She didn't suppose for a moment that he had been celibate since his wife died. Men didn't deny themselves—but she had, for years, without realising it.

Now William had opened the floodgates of her sensuality, and she was desperate to see where it could take her, to explore the uncharted waters of her womanhood.

So she nodded.

The flash of desire on his lean features was her reward. His fingers threaded through hers and he led her briskly across the grass to the car park.

'What about the others?' she asked him breathlessly.

'What about them? You want a party?'

She laughed. 'No—I just thought we ought to say goodbye.'

He snorted softly. 'No way, José. There's enough speculation about us without exposing you to any more. Let them wonder where we've gone.'

He seated her in the car then went round and slid behind the wheel, his shoulder brushing hers as he leant in and slammed the door.

Minutes later they were pulling up outside his house, and she found herself in the hall, her heart in her mouth. Suddenly she was scared—more scared than she had ever been in her life, and terrifyingly, desperately afraid of failure.

What if she couldn't respond? What if last Saturday had been a fluke? Blindly she stared down at her feet, wishing herself almost anywhere else in the world.

Then his arms were round her. 'What is it?' he asked.

'I feel so silly,' she mumbled. 'I'm scared.'

His hands kneaded her spine gently. 'Don't be,' he told her, his voice soft. 'There's nothing to be afraid of.'

'I'll disappoint you.'

'Rubbish.'

'I'm no good.'

'Charlotte?'

'I'm no——'

'Charlotte.'

She looked up at him then. 'Yes?'

'Shut up,' he said softly, and his lips settled on hers, silencing her.

It was an undemanding kiss, gentle and generous, warming her right down to the soles of her feet. When he lifted his head and stared down at her, she felt the tenderness in his eyes like armour, gathering round her, protecting her.

He led her into the sitting-room and closed the curtains, then put on some music, soothing and relaxing. Clearly he had no intention of hustling her off to bed with undue haste, she realised, and then almost found herself wishing he would, just to get it over with.

He sat on the sofa and patted the space beside him, but she went to the other end and sat stiffly, twisting her fingers together.

He sighed. 'Charlotte, for God's sake, trust me.'

She looked up at him, startled. 'I trust you,' she said. 'It's me I've got the problem with.'

He closed the gap. Instead of trying to coax her up to his end, he swung his legs round on to the arm and lay down with his head in her lap, gazing up at her. 'There. Now if I step out of line all you have to do is bonk me on the nose and I'll behave,' he told her, and she laughed, despite her nerves.

'That's better,' he said approvingly, and, closing his eyes, he reached up and pulled the clip off her hair. It flowed round her shoulders, and he threaded his fingers through it and sighed. 'Feels lovely,' he murmured, and, turning his face towards her, he pressed a kiss to the soft curve of her breast. His sigh was deep and lazy and self-satisfied. 'You smell wonderful,' he told her. 'Sexy and mysterious and wanton.'

'You wish.'

He grinned and opened his eyes. 'You are at night— in my dreams. All this repression vanishes, giving way to a seductive siren whose whole *raison d'être* is driving me to distraction.'

She blushed. 'Don't hold your breath,' she told him, now more than ever convinced that she would disappoint him when the moment came. After all, she had failed before, for years——

'It just gives me something to aim for,' he said softly. 'Besides, anyone can dream.'

She stared down into his eyes. Was it true? Could she allow herself to dream? To pretend, at least for a while, that everything was all right?

'Would you do something for me?' she asked hesitantly. 'Would you just—hold me?'

He stood up, swung her legs up on to the sofa and lay down beside her, wrapping her in his arms.

'Better?'

She snuggled closer. 'Much.'

'Mmm.'

For a long while they were silent, then he sighed and Charlotte opened her eyes.

'Are you tired?'

He laughed softly. 'I'm always tired, but the last couple of weeks have been particularly busy with the old man away on holiday.'

'When does he come back?' she asked.

He groaned. 'Monday—don't, I'm dreading it. For all there's more to do without him, in so many ways it's easier. He'll start interfering and getting out the scissors, and all the midwives will be on strike—it's unbearable.'

She threaded her fingers through his hair and smoothed it back from his face. 'Is he really so awful?'

'Oh, God, horrendous. He's rooted in the Stone Age—well, no, that's a lie. If he were rooted in the Stone Age he'd be a lot better! No, he's stuck firmly in America of the late seventies, with interventionist technology and the bedside manner of a rabid gorilla.'

Charlotte laughed, and he opened his eyes. 'It isn't funny. He really is bad, so bad that off the record I can't believe he hasn't got the push. Thank God for his inherent idleness, that's all I can say. He applies the word "consultant" to the nth degree. His constant absence is his only saving grace.'

'Because it gives Dr Ventouse the opportunity to practice gentle, safe childbirth techniques?'

He snorted softly. 'Because it gives the women the opportunity, never mind me. If anyone goes into labour during the afternoon, the midwives always keep quiet until they hear his shoes squeak off the ward. Then they run and find me if there's a problem. Only if it's really critical will they say anything while he's kicking around.'

Charlotte's fingers sifted idly through his hair, enjoying the silky texture. 'How old is he?' she asked lazily.

'About a hundred and five, but he says he's only sixty-four.'

'So he's going to go soon?'

'Mmm. Don't stop, that feels wonderful.'

She looked up into his eyes, just inches from hers, and he closed the gap. Their lips met, and he nibbled gently and sighed. 'You taste of ketchup.'

She licked the corner of his mouth. 'So do you.'

'Messy eaters.'

'Mmm.'

His lips brushed hers again, then again, and then settled with a contented sigh. She felt the tip of his tongue trace the seam of her lips and parted them, allowing him access. She expected him to deepen the kiss instantly, but he didn't, instead playing with her lips, licking and nibbling and gently teasing. Her hands were trapped against his chest, and she discovered that his shirt closed with snaps, not buttons.

He eased his mouth away as she tugged the shirt open. 'I wore it deliberately,' he told her. 'I knew you wouldn't be able to keep your hands off me, and I can't afford to let you wreck my entire wardrobe.'

She giggled and blushed guiltily. 'I'm sorry about that.'

'Don't worry, it was worth it.'

'Worth it?' she said, amazed. 'What did you get out of it?'

'Watching you,' he told her quietly. 'Holding you, giving you pleasure.'

She blushed again. 'I still can't believe I let you do that,' she mumbled into his chest.

'I can—it's played havoc with my sleep,' he told her, and under her hands his chest shook with rueful laughter.

She smoothed her palms over his ribcage, fascinated by the contrast of soft skin with dense, wiry curls. The almost black hair covered the centre of his chest between the flat copper coins of his nipples, narrowing down to dart enticingly under the waistband of his jeans. She traced the hair with the tip of a finger, and

was gratified to see his midriff clench. She flattened
her hand and slid it beneath the edge of his jeans,
following that tantalising trail of curls. His breath
hissed through his teeth and his hand came down and
shackled her wrist, easing it away.

'No?' she said softly.

'No, because you aren't ready for this and there's a
limit to what I can take.'

She stared at him in amazement. 'Not ready? But I
thought—aren't we. . .?'

He shook his head. 'No. Not tonight, at least.' He
swung his feet to the floor and stood up, pulling her
to her feet. 'Come on, I'll take you home.'

She went—confused, frustrated and just the tiniest
bit relieved.

CHAPTER FOUR

DEREK BLYTHE, the bane of William's life, drifted into the department on Monday looking tanned, dapper and swaggeringly confident.

'Managed without me?' he boomed, and the staff nurse on duty gave a weak smile.

'We seem to have coped, sir,' William said drily.

'The old man' harrumphed and turned on his heel.

'I'll be in my office—paperwork to deal with,' he threw over his shoulder, and as his shoes squeaked out of earshot, so everyone heaved a sigh of relief.

Charlotte wondered if they were all exaggerating, but on Tuesday night when she and William were on call again she discovered that they were all in deadly earnest.

'If she doesn't have that baby by the time Blythe comes back in the morning, he'll have her in Theatre,' William told Charlotte as they left the delivery suite.

A woman in her late thirties was in labour for the first time, and was making steady but very slow progress. She seemed reluctant to try the water pool and simply wanted to lie down and wait for it all to happen, but Sue was desperate to get her moving.

The problem was how to do so without worrying her, especially as her husband wasn't with her but had had to go home to look after the young children from his first marriage.

They went into the ward office and William produced a pack of cards.

'Do you play cards?' he asked.

'What, like bridge?' she said doubtfully.

'Nah—fun cards—like slap.'

'Slap?'

'Yeah—like snap but quieter. You have to slap the cards if they're the same, and the object is to win all the cards.'

She smiled. 'I think I can almost manage to remember the rules for that,' she told him.

They played, and he won, of course. Then he won the next.

'Best of five?' she said, determined not to be beaten so easily.

She won the next game after a long and hilarious tussle, and then the next. With the last game, when he seemed to be making no attempt to slap the cards, she slapped his hands instead.

'You aren't supposed to let me win,' she told him laughingly, and looked up to surprise a curious expression on his face. 'William?' she said softly.

His eyes locked on hers. 'I'm sorry,' he murmured. 'I was distracted—you looked so lovely, laughing and relaxed, having fun—do you know that's the first time I've ever really heard you laugh?'

She looked away, then back. 'Don't be silly,' she whispered.

'I'm not. I mean it; you don't laugh nearly enough.'

'Maybe I don't have very much to laugh about,' she said quietly.

He was silent for a moment, then he said, 'We'll have to do something about that, won't we?' but his light tone was at odds with the intensity of his eyes.

She put the cards down and reached blindly for his

hand, and for an endless moment they sat there, unable to look away from each other.

Then he seemed to pull himself together and pushed back his chair. 'I'll go and check on our patient—you might make us a cup of tea.'

Then he was gone, leaving her with a warm glow round her heart and his promise ringing in her ears.

So what if she couldn't have forever? She could have now, couldn't she? Nobody was talking about anything permanent. Other people had affairs. Maybe it was time she did, too. As William had said only the other night, 'anyone can dream'.

If only she could be sure she wouldn't make a fool of herself. . .

They went to gynae later and she clerked the new admission while he went up to Theatre to prepare for her operation. She had an ectopic pregnancy, and William was reluctant to leave her till the morning in case it ruptured.

Charlotte watched him operate, more for information than because she would ever need to do it, and then once he was happy they went back down to the maternity ward to see how their other patient was progressing.

Slowly, was the short answer.

'She won't listen to me when I tell her to get up. Perhaps she'll pay more attention to you as you're a doctor,' Sue said.

With a shrug William perched on the edge of the bed and took the sleepy woman's hand.

'Mrs Greaves? Can I have a word with you about your labour?'

She roused herself and blinked. 'Oh, sure. Sorry, I dozed off.'

William smiled. 'It all seems to be going rather slowly, doesn't it?'

She nodded. 'Is that bad?'

William shrugged. 'No, not really, but if it goes on too long your baby could become very tired and distressed. I'd like to see if we can speed it up a bit.'

'Oh, I don't want a drip,' she said, her eyes widening with horror.

'OK. I think that's reasonable at the moment. However, if we can't get you speeded up, it may be necessary in the end.'

She struggled into a sitting position. 'So how do you want to speed it up? Rupture my membranes?'

He shook his head. 'No. I'd rather they were left intact for now. No, I think if you can get up and walk around with Sue's help, and then maybe try the water pool—that's been known to speed things up a lot and reduce pain at the same time. Now, I know you're reluctant to give birth in the water, but I think for the purposes of your labour it could be beneficial. You can always come out for the end.'

'Oh. Right.'

She looked very doubtful, but Sue helped her up and started walking her about, and William and Charlotte went back into the ward kitchen.

'Tea?' he suggested.

'Lovely. What will happen if she doesn't speed up?'

He snorted. 'The old man'll put her on oxytocin and a continuous fetal monitor and at the first dip in heart-rate will rupture her membranes, cut her from ear to ear and yank the poor little object out with forceps—or do a section. He'll claim it's for the baby's sake, but personally I think he's frightened of litigation.'

'And you aren't?'

He grinned. 'I'm well-insured—but what I'm trying to do is encourage women to do what their bodies were designed for. I know babies are bigger than they used to be, and women are generally older and less fit, but, with active encouragement and the judicious use of vacuum assistance when absolutely necessary, the vast majority give birth with no trouble at all.'

'What about the ones that can't?' Charlotte asked.

He grinned. 'You think I leave them to struggle?'

'No. I can't imagine you would, but where do you draw the line?'

'With individuals, but there are some conditions which there's no flexibility on, and I know that. I do sections for low placental placement, antepartum haemorrhage or premature elective delivery for detected maternal or fetal abnormality, like an obstructed gut, gastroschisis and so on, for multiple pregnancy or if the baby is clearly distressed and there's no other safe way.

'Not,' he added with a grin, 'because the day's dragging and I want to get home!'

Charlotte glanced at the clock on the wall. 'It's nearly five,' she told him.

'Mmm. I know. She's got four hours before he comes back. I just hope it's enough.'

He swallowed the last of his tea and then stood up. 'Come for a stroll round the garden.'

There was a courtyard garden behind the maternity block, with a little pool and fountain, and they went down in the lift and out into the cool morning air. It was slightly misty, and the sun was just edging over the trees in the distance.

'It's gorgeous,' Charlotte sighed. 'Fresh and cool and beautiful.'

'Mmm—like you.'

She turned towards him, and her breath lodged in her throat. His eyes were shielded, but a muscle worked at the corner of his jaw and there was something about the set of his mouth.

'I want to kiss you,' he murmured, his voice almost lost in the cool of the morning, and she stepped closer. There was no thought of denying him, because it would have meant denying herself and she found she couldn't.

Their hands met and clung, and, bending his head, he touched his lips to hers. 'Charlotte,' he breathed, and then his mouth grew more urgent. She parted her lips and he deepened the kiss, his tongue stroking, delving, tormenting until she could hardly breathe.

Their bodies shifted closer together, and she could feel the hard ridge of his arousal. She moaned and leant into him, and her action drew an answering groan from deep in his chest. Then he lifted his head, his hands still entwined with hers, and stared deep into her eyes. His thumbs caressed her absent-mindedly.

'I want you,' he said gruffly. 'You know that, don't you?'

She nodded, her heart pounding.

'Not yet, but soon. When you're ready.'

I'm ready now! her body screamed, but her mind knew he was right, and sex, as she knew only too well, was much more about the mind than the body. At least, that was true for women, and she suspected it might be true for William too.

She stepped back away from him, although her body

ached to lean into his and absorb him through her skin, so close did she want to be to him.

They went back up to the maternity ward and found their patient, Mrs Greaves, just getting into the water pool with Sue's assistance.

'Things are looking up,' Sue said cheerfully over her shoulder, and William, catching Charlotte's eye, glanced down at himself and grinned. She blushed, and he ran his tongue over the edge of his teeth, his shoulders shaking with silent laughter.

Winking wickedly, he moved over to the side of the pool and squatted down. 'Hello, Mrs Greaves,' he said cheerfully. 'How does the water feel?'

'Oh—warm, soothing—lovely. I can't think why I didn't like the idea.'

They stayed for a while, long enough to see that her contractions were stronger and she was progressing well, and then William was bleeped.

'They need one of us in A and E—want to come?' he asked Charlotte.

'What about Mrs Greaves?'

'She's fine for a while. Come on—then we'll go and have a cup of coffee and a bite in the canteen; I'm starving.'

'You're always starving,' she told him candidly, and he grinned.

'A man with an appetite,' he said, but he wasn't talking about food.

Charlotte's heart thumped.

At precisely five to nine, in the water and with a minimum of fuss, Mrs Greaves gave birth to a lovely, healthy baby boy. Her husband had returned to the hospital following Sue's phone call and was there for the birth, and although it wasn't the first time he'd been through it he was nevertheless overjoyed.

Sue had just clamped and cut the cord and helped Mrs Greaves out of the water when the door swung open and Derek Blythe squeaked in.

'Mrs Greaves delivered yet, or are you determined to lose the baby?' he growled, and marched past them. William could hardly contain his smug smile as they watched him go into the birthing centre, and as the man emerged and left the ward again Charlotte was sure she heard William chuckle.

'Why doesn't his wife chuck out those awful shoes?' the staff nurse said under her breath. 'Squeak, squeak —aogh!'

Charlotte laughed, the lightening of tension affecting her too.

William shook his head. 'That was a close shave— good job Sue got her moving. Right, talking of close shaves, I'm going to have a shower and attack this stubble and I'll be back—we've got an antenatal clinic. Could you go down and get things under way?'

'Don't I need a shower?' she asked mildly.

'Very likely, but at least you don't look as if you've slept in the hedge.' He ran his hand ruefully over his chin and grinned. 'Five minutes—promise.'

She snorted, and went down to the clinic. One of the first patients was Jennifer Barrett, the paediatric consultant's wife, and Charlotte found her husband in the examination-room with her. She knew him well, having done six months on Paediatrics with him, and she had found him an excellent teacher and a deeply compassionate man. She was sure he would be a superb father to his own children, unlike some of the parents she had met in the past few weeks.

He greeted her with a welcoming smile. 'Hi—how's it going?'

'Oh, great,' she told him. 'Good—except that babies seem to like being born at night!'

Andrew laughed. 'Yes, well, I hope this one isn't unless William Parry's on call. Jennifer's determined to have him around just in case.'

Jennifer smiled. 'His reputation precedes him. I have a friend who got into difficulties and had a ventouse delivery, and she says he's got the longest and most skilful fingers of any gynaecologist she's ever met— and that's probably the most significant qualification!'

Charlotte laughed, covering her mouth with her hand to stifle her mirth, and Andrew squirmed with embarrassment, but Jennifer was cheerfully unrepentant.

'Are you expecting problems?' Charlotte asked her, but she shook her head.

'My first delivery was fine,' she said, 'so no, I don't expect any problems, but Andrew is a lot bigger than my first husband so if it takes after him—well, it could make things a little trickier.'

Charlotte nodded. 'Babies seem to fit the mother, more often than not,' she said, 'but we'll do a scan to check. How many weeks are you now?'

'Thirty-seven.'

'OK, we'd better do that this morning. Let's just check everything else and then we'll send you out to drink gallons and get uncomfy before they scan you!'

'Oh, great, I can hardly wait,' she said with a laugh, and, lying down, she let Charlotte take her blood-pressure, listen to her chest and palpate her abdomen.

'It feels like a lovely position,' she said, 'but William will be down in a minute and he can check it; I'd rather be on the safe side. At the moment my diagnostic skills in obstetrics are a bit limited.'

She heard his voice then, and, sticking her head round the door, she called to him.

'Can you come and have a look at Mrs Barrett?' she asked, and he nodded. As he walked past her she caught the fresh tang of soap and saw the faint gleam of taut skin on his jaw where he had freshly shaved, and her gut clenched.

Why, oh, why does he affect me like this? she asked herself.

William chatted briefly to the couple as he washed his hands and tugged on gloves, then Jennifer made a wisecrack about his long fingers and he chuckled.

'That's me—the best hands in the business. Right, let's see how this baby's getting on, shall we?'

Using his right hand to examine her internally, he used the palm of his left hand over the curve of the baby's bottom to push it down and test the fit of the occiput against the pelvic brim.

'No problem,' he said with satisfaction. 'We'll scan you anyway, but there's tons of room and it's not going to grow any more. Your cervix is very ripe— it's probably beginning to dilate, in fact. Was Tim early?'

She nodded. 'A little—four days, I think.'

'Right. Well, let's scan and see what we come up with, and then you'd better go home and pack, because I don't, frankly, think you've got long.'

Andrew laughed ruefully. 'Can't you stall her a bit? We really don't need an early baby—we only got married on Christmas Eve!'

William glanced at his watch. 'Seventeenth of August—hmm. Early honeymoon?'

Jennifer spluttered with laughter. 'You could say that.'

Andrew sighed. 'Oh, well, it'll give me a bit more street cred. She's packed, anyway. She's been packed for weeks. I'll see if Anne can hang on to Tim for a while.'

'Wait a minute,' Jennifer said, flapping her hand at him. 'Why so fast? I mean, surely we've got a day or so?'

William raised an eyebrow. 'I'll bet you ten pounds your baby arrives before midnight.'

She sighed. 'Are you on call tonight?'

He grinned. 'I am now—only do me a favour. Last night was a long one. Could you get a bit of a hustle on? In fact, if you have it before nine, I'll give *you* ten pounds.'

The Barretts' baby, a beautiful little girl, was actually born at four-thirty that afternoon, with no fuss and bother and without William's attention.

He was very disappointed. 'I almost wanted to do a ventouse on her to prove how good I am,' he joked.

'I used to be modest but I'm perfect now,' Charlotte said with a straight face.

A slight smile played around his eyes. 'Are you getting at me?' he asked plaintively.

She raised an eyebrow. 'Would I?'

He snorted. 'Oh, well, I'm going to go and have a cuddle with the little sweetheart anyway. Coming?'

She went, if only for the bittersweet pleasure of seeing him with a child in his arms.

Jennifer had been moved to a little side-ward, and when they went in Andrew was sitting in the easy-chair, his tiny daughter tucked into the crook of his arm, smiling the biggest smile Charlotte had ever seen.

'She's amazing,' he said, over and over again. 'So gorgeous.'

'Takes after you, darling,' Jennifer said with a wink, and he snorted.

'Poor child, don't be nasty to her on her first day. Mummy's being mean, isn't she, darling?' he crooned, and the baby made a sleepy little noise and relaxed against him.

'I want a cuddle,' William told him.

'With me or the baby?' Andrew asked drily.

'Well, you really, but I'll settle for the baby,' he said with a grin, and, bending over, he slid his hands under the small body and lifted her carefully into his arms.

Charlotte's heart ached as she watched him staring down into the tiny little face. Oh, God, she thought, I'm falling for him. It would be so easy to pretend the baby was theirs, that he had every right to hold her like that.

He stroked the downy velvet cheek with one long, blunt finger. 'You cheated me,' he told her seriously. 'I wanted to see you being born.'

Her eyes opened and she stared up at him for a second, then her little face puckered and she let out a wail.

'Such flattery,' he murmured, and reluctantly handed her over to her mother.

'So, how do you feel?' he asked Jennifer.

'Shell-shocked. I didn't have the first twinge till three-thirty.'

'That's the way to do it,' William said with a grin, and, bending forward, he dropped a kiss on Jennifer's bent head. 'I owe you ten pounds—I'm going home for an early night,' he said, the grin widening, and, placing a gentle hand on Charlotte's back, he ushered her out into the corridor.

'Are you OK?' he asked her.

She smiled wearily. 'Yes—tired, but I'll live.'

'Me too—I feel bushwacked.' They walked together to the entrance by the staff car park, then paused, reluctant to part.

'Come home with me,' he said suddenly. 'I'm too tired to be a threat, but I just want to hold you.'

She looked at him, his eyes red-rimmed, his mouth drawn, and shook her head. It was too, too tempting, and what she really needed was twelve hours' straight, uninterrupted sleep and time to marshal her thoughts.

'I'll see you in the morning,' she promised, and he sighed and nodded.

'You're probably right. Goodnight, Charlotte. Sleep well.'

'Goodnight.'

She was just about to turn and walk away when he drew her into his arms and kissed her.

By the time he let her go, any chance of a good night's sleep had vanished without trace.

She dreamed of him that night—wild and vivid dreams, and then others, tender, poignant, from which she woke with tears on her cheeks and an aching sense of loss.

She had always thought envy was a destructive emotion, and she was right. Day after day she watched ecstatic couples like the Barretts greeting their babies for the first time, and day after day the envy ate away at her.

It wasn't vicious, just a gentle, insidious ache

that left her even more lonely than before.

She wanted—no, needed—to share it with William, to unburden herself and so ease the load, but he was the very last person she could talk to. Anyway, she didn't think she could put it into words, because it was a pain she couldn't share—any more than he could share his pain. He had still told her nothing about his wife, or her death. It was a subject kept strictly under wraps, a pain to be nursed alone, in secret.

She knew all about that.

Their affair, if they ever reached that point, could never be more than that because she thought too much of him to want to short-change him, and she was no bargain.

Anyway, she thought, it was unlikely to be a problem. For now he seemed a little fascinated by her. Once they had made love, no doubt his interest would quickly wane. He was too skilled, too physical, too sensuous to settle for someone so hopelessly inept.

But she could dream. Even he had said so.

And so she did—and woke with tears on her cheeks, and an ache in her heart that not even William— perhaps especially not William—could take away. And she wondered about his pain, and longed to be able to ease it for him.

Two weeks later, when she was on call over the weekend, she was called urgently down to A and E for a pregnant woman who had been stabbed.

'We need William Parry,' she told the duty doctor, overwhelmed by the magnitude of the woman's injuries. 'He's at home—get the switchboard to call him, please.'

The phone rang seconds later. He was on his way,

and the patient, a woman in her early thirties, was prepared for Theatre as fast as possible. Blood was taken for crossmatching and she was given two units of plasma expander stat, before being transferred to the maternity theatre where William had just finished scrubbing.

'What's the problem?' he asked.

'Heavily pregnant woman been stabbed in the abdomen—there's a good strong heartbeat from the baby, but her blood-pressure's dropping fast.'

'Right. Someone page a paediatrician and a general surgeon—I want them here now. Let's get her opened up and get that baby out, and then perhaps we can find out what's going on.'

There was no thought of why or how or where she had been stabbed. That was a matter for the police. For Charlotte and William and the rest of the surgical team, the priority was getting the baby out and halting the mother's bleeding while they were both still alive.

She had never seen such a rapid Caesarian section. As soon as the uterus was opened William lifted the baby out and handed it to the waiting midwife, and then, moving the uterus out of the way, he peered into the opened abdomen.

'My God, it's a bloodbath,' he muttered. 'Let's have some suction, please—not there! Right, that's better—oh, hell, it's a renal artery; she must have been stabbed in the back as well.'

Reaching in, he grasped the artery in his hand and crushed it flat, and the gush of blood slowed to a steady well.

Ross Hamilton arrived at that moment, and took over the stab wound to the renal artery while William traced and sutured another lower down in her abdomen. By a miracle her bowel was untouched, and, judging by the yelling from the other side of the room, the baby was alive and kicking.

As they worked to save the mother, Charlotte became aware of an unaccustomed tension in William, a grim stillness about his face that worried her.

Finally they had done all they could and closed the abdomen, and she was taken through to Recovery prior to being transferred to ITU. The baby was to go down to SCBU in Andrew Barrett's care.

'How is it?' William asked him tersely, tugging off his gloves.

'Oh, fine. Tiny nick on one arm—nothing to worry about. I've put some Steristrips on to hold it together, rather than stitch it. Otherwise the baby's fine. Looks almost term, actually. Any relatives about?'

William shrugged his shoulders. 'Ask Charlotte. I wasn't there.'

He left the theatre and went to the changing-rooms, ripping off his gown and mask as he went. Charlotte saw his face for the first time since they had arrived in Theatre, and the grim look on it shocked her to the core. What had distressed him so much? He had handled emergencies before without the slightest ruffling of his composure.

She was desperate to find out but she was unable to talk to him while he changed. Instead she showered and changed herself, and went back down to the ward to find William in there, slouched in the kitchen with a mug in his hand.

Jake Hunter, Alex Carter's SR, was in there too, and his face was equally grim.

'So it was the ex-husband?' William was saying.

'So I gather. The police have got him in custody,

anyway. The baby's father's in SCBU making his son's acquaintance, and waiting anxiously to hear if his wife's going to make it.'

A spasm of pain crossed William's face. 'She should,' he said gruffly, and, reaching out, he filled a mug with tea and handed it to Charlotte.

'Here—you look as if you need it.'

Charlotte nearly laughed. If she looked as if she needed tea, God alone knows what he looked like. She eyed him worriedly. 'Are you OK?' she asked, her voice soft.

'I'll live,' he grunted. He slapped the mug down on the worktop, and with a muttered, 'Excuse me,' he squeezed past her and left the room.

She turned to Jake. 'Is there something wrong? Something I don't know about?' she asked.

Jake's mouth tensed into a grim line. 'You'd better ask him that.'

Jake moved to go past her but she stilled him with a hand on his arm. 'Something to do with his wife?'

Jake's eyes were kindly and concerned. 'You'll have to ask him—but I would say this probably isn't a good moment.'

She nodded. 'OK—thanks.'

She watched Jake's retreating back, and sighed. She was tied to the hospital all weekend, and by Monday night she would be exhausted. Tuesday, then, at the earliest, but she would ask him—she had to, because she had seen the agony in his eyes and couldn't let him carry it alone.

By Tuesday evening she was wondering if she dared intrude. The woman was out of danger and had been transferred to the maternity ward, her baby was with her and her ex-husband was in police custody. But

William was still as remote as ever, and for once seemed reluctant to go and grab his usual cuddles with the babies.

Maybe she had no right to ask. Some things were too deep to talk about, too painful and too private to share.

She had to try, though. She had to, because she loved him. Maybe she could just give him silent, unde-manding support.

She arrived at his house unannounced, and at first she thought he was out, but then finally she saw him through the leaded lights in the door, striding towards her. The door opened and he stood for a second, staring at her.

'Hi,' he said finally, but his voice sounded rusty and unused.

'Hi. May I come in?'

He nodded slowly. 'Yes, of course. I'm sorry, I'm a bit. . .'

He closed the door and led her down to the conserva-tory. There was an unopened bottle of whisky on the table, and a glass.

She stared at it in surprise. 'I'm sorry, have you got guests coming?'

'No.'

'But the whisky—you don't drink.'

'I used to,' he said tersely. 'I was just thinking about starting again. What do you want, Charlotte?'

She grasped her courage in both hands. 'To talk to you—help you, maybe. I don't know what it is, but you look so—alone, so hurt. I wanted to help.'

His jaw worked, and he turned away, staring down the garden, hands thrust in the pockets of his trousers.

'There's nothing you can do.'

'I can listen.'

'Can you?' he asked. 'It isn't pretty.'

She stood and walked over to him, laying a hand on his shoulder. 'I didn't think it would be, somehow.'

He was silent for a long moment, then he let his breath out on a ragged sigh.

'Five years ago my wife was shot, getting money out of the cashpoint to pay for some nursery equipment. She was nine months pregnant with my son. I lost them both to a trigger-happy teenage junkie, for a miserable fifty pounds.'

CHAPTER FIVE

CHARLOTTE had expected something like this. After all, William had warned her it wasn't pretty.

But, even so, his quiet statement chilled her and she felt shock drain the blood from her face.

Words seemed inadequate, but still she needed to try and reach him. She squeezed gently with her fingers on his shoulder. 'Oh, William—I'm so, so sorry,' she said quietly.

'It's OK,' he told her. 'I'm used to it now; I've worked through my grief and come to terms with it. I still miss Eleanor at times, but not like I did, not with that awful, raw ache. It's just something like this brings it all back as if it were yesterday. . .'

He turned towards her and gave a fleeting smile. 'Hence the Scotch. It's been there since Saturday evening. I keep staring at it.'

She nodded, understanding. 'Sort of anaesthetic—a pain-killer, just in case it gets too much and you need to block it out.'

'No—more of a test, to see how far I've come.'

He picked it up in his hands and turned it over, studying it, then walked to the sink, unscrewed the cap and up-ended it over the plughole.

The simple symbolic gesture made her want to cry. 'Well done,' she said, and, crossing over to him, she wrapped her arms around his waist and hugged him.

He turned in her arms, dropping his head against hers and cradling her against his chest.

'I've needed you so much,' he said gruffly. 'I don't think I've ever felt so alone in my life as I have these last few days.'

He led her into the conservatory and they sat together side by side on the little wicker settee, his arm round her shoulders, his other hand clasped between hers on her lap.

'Tell me about it?' she asked.

'You don't really want to hear it.'

'Do you want to talk it through?'

He sighed. 'Maybe I should. I need to tell you anyway—you ought to know.'

She waited, and after a while he began to speak.

'I was twenty-eight, Eleanor was twenty-six. We'd been married for three years, since I was in my final year and she was a staff nurse on one of my wards.'

'Was she pretty?' Charlotte asked, hating herself but needing to know.

'Not especially—average height, average build, mousy hair—but I loved her. I loved her desperately. She was sweet and funny and I missed her like hell.'

He swallowed, and paused for a moment before continuing. 'The baby was planned—I was an SHO, I had a registrar's job lined up—the timing was just right. We bought a little house and did it up in our spare time, which wasn't much. Then Eleanor took maternity leave and I started my new job. She rang me one day, and said there was some nursery equipment in the paper, should she go and look at it. I said yes, and she did, and the woman apparently asked for cash.

'Eleanor went to the cashpoint to draw it out, in broad daylight, and this kid jumped her. God knows where he'd got the gun from. There were several witnesses, but he got away and he was never caught.

It's probably just as well, because I think I would have killed him with my bare hands.'

Charlotte looked down at his hand, clenched between her open palms, and smoothed it with her fingers. Gradually it relaxed and his fingers opened, threading through hers.

'She was brought into A and E and rushed up to Theatre. She was still alive, but they brought the baby out to me. He was dead—unmarked, but one of the bullets had severed the umbilical cord. What a freak of fate.'

His fingers tightened on hers, and she increased the pressure, giving him wordless comfort.

'He was beautiful. Quite perfect. He had masses of dark hair, and his fingers and toes were so tiny and delicate they were almost transparent. He was still warm, and it didn't seem possible that he wasn't alive.'

'Did they try and resuscitate him?'

'I think so. I'm not sure. It didn't work if they did. I sat outside the theatre and held him while they worked on her. Finally they came and told me they'd lost her on the table. Her aorta had been nicked, and it had ruptured. Her blood-pressure was already so low from loss of blood volume that her circulation just collapsed. They did what they could, but——'

He broke off, his eyes closed, then gave a shuddering sigh. 'I'm sorry; I'm normally OK when I talk about it, but just since this happened——'

She held his hand, her head resting against his chest, and let the silence stretch. Gradually the tension left him and he eased his grip on her hand. She flexed her fingers.

'I'm sorry, was I hurting you?'

She shook her head. 'No. I'm fine. How about you?'

He gave her a fleeting smile. 'Oh, I'm OK. Just sad. It's the baby. It was funny; after the funeral I hit the bottle in a big way. I didn't go out except to the off licence, I didn't go to work—my new boss came to see me and I told him where to get off. When I came to about six months later, my job was gone. Surprise, surprise. So I started applying for other jobs, and eventually I got one.'

He laughed. 'Despite my appalling behaviour and unspeakable rudeness, he gave me a fantastic reference, apparently. Anyway, to cut a long story short I thought I was making good progress with my grieving. I settled into my new job, then two years later I moved here to the SR's job. I thought I was fine, but then I started talking to someone about it, and she asked how I'd coped with losing the baby.'

'And?' she prompted.

'I started to cry. I cried for about two weeks, and then gave away all the nursery stuff I'd kept, put myself back together again and went on with my life.'

'When was that?'

'Just over two years ago. It was Jo Carter. She'd lost a baby—an ectopic pregnancy. Did you know they couldn't have children? She had to have a hysterectomy.'

Charlotte felt a dart of pain deep inside. 'No,' she said numbly. 'I didn't. I thought they had a little girl?'

'They have—Amy. She's adopted.'

'But it's not the same,' Charlotte said quietly.

'No. They love her, though, just as if she were their own child.'

'It must hurt, being in obstetrics, with all those constant reminders.'

'They run the infertility clinic as well. I guess it gives them an extra insight.'

'I'm sure,' Charlotte agreed. 'How sad for them.'

'Mmm.' He tugged her closer and dropped a kiss on her brow. 'Fancy a stroll round the garden in the moonlight?'

She nodded, shaking off her melancholy. 'Yes, I do. I can smell something wonderful.'

'Nicotiana—tobacco plants. They come up every year just under the conservatory windows, and smell fantastic in the evening. There are some night-scented stocks as well, and lilac in the spring—all sorts of smellies. My mother knows I like fragrant things. All the roses are scented. Come on, I'll walk you round.'

The garden was, indeed, a mass of scents in the quiet night. The musky perfume of old-fashioned roses, the deeply intoxicating scent of the stocks and nicotiana, the late Belgian honeysuckle. . .

'It's wonderful,' she breathed.

They paused under a tree, their faces shadowed by the leafy canopy, and he drew her into his arms.

'Thanks for being there for me, for caring enough to ask what was wrong.'

'Oh, William,' she said unsteadily, and then his lips found hers and clung, the heat blossoming like wildfire in their veins.

After a while she pushed him away, a sobering thought in her mind.

'I'm not Eleanor,' she reminded him.

'Oh, Charlotte, I know you're not Eleanor,' he said gently. 'I'm over her, truly. I'm ready to move on. I have been for some time.' He caressed her face tenderly. 'How about you? Are you ready to move on?'

Desire, hot and sweet, coursed through her veins.

She could never move on—there was nowhere to go—but here, with William, on this glorious scented night, surely she could dream?

She reached up a trembling hand and touched his face, and he turned his head and pressed a hot, wild kiss into her palm. Her knees sagged and she gasped, and the next second she was in his arms and he was striding towards the house, his face taut with desire.

He carried her in, up through the house to a large bedroom at the back overlooking the garden. The window was open and the scents of the night drifted on the air, rich and intoxicating.

He didn't switch on the light, but he left the curtains open so that the moonlight streamed in and gleamed silver on his hair. He took off his shirt and threw it aside, then came back to her, lifting her T-shirt over her head and sighing raggedly as his hands found her small, aching breasts.

'God, you're so exquisite,' he whispered, freeing them, but her demons were still there, taunting her.

'I don't have a bust,' she told him.

He swore, softly but succinctly, then his head swooped and he drew one nipple right into his mouth, suckling deeply. Her legs buckled and he caught her, lifting her and laying her in the middle of a great big four-poster bed. The moonlight gleamed on his shoulders, glazing him with white fire, and she reached out and touched him in wonder.

'You look like some kind of god, cast in silver,' she told him, her fingers trailing over his shoulder and down across his chest.

He caught her hand and turned it palm up, kissing it, licking it with his tongue and sucking each finger in turn. She moaned softly, and he stripped off the rest of their clothes and came back to lie beside her, his body hard and warm against hers, not silver at all but real flesh and blood and bone and sinew.

Now, she thought. Now he'll make love to me, and then he'll know.

Her eyes filled with tears, but she blinked them away. Maybe she could fake her response—could she fool him? No, probably not; he knew too much. Oh, well.

But to her surprise he did nothing more than cup her chin in his hand and kiss her lingeringly.

'Are you OK?' he asked after a minute, and she nodded.

Now, then.

No.

He cupped her breast, his hand warm and gentle, and nuzzled it with his lips. Fire danced in her veins, and she moaned softly. His hand slid down her flank, round over her thigh, trailing fire in its wake.

Now, surely to God.

But he moved on, his hand never lingering, stroking behind her knee, over her thigh and up again, across her flank, round behind her to cup the soft flesh of her bottom and pull her towards him as his mouth trailed hot, open-mouthed kisses over her waist and round into the sensitive bowl of her pelvis, in the dip between her hipbones.

She cried out, a faint keening noise, and he growled with satisfaction. His hand came round again, pausing on the damp nest of curls to dip and delve, making her shake with need.

Surely now—please, God, surely now——

'Patience, patience,' he murmured, and she realised she had spoken aloud.

His hand was moving now, slowly, rhythmically, and she bucked beneath it, her whole body trembling.

'Please—oh, now, William, please.'

'No,' he told her.

'Why?' Her voice was a sob. 'Why torment me? Don't do this again, please. I couldn't bear it again without you. Why do it if you don't want me?'

His hand stilled and he moved against her, leaving her in no doubt.

'Of course I want you—I want you so badly I can taste it,' he grated, 'but I'm so close, so very, very close, and I'm damned if I'm going anywhere without you.'

'Oh, William,' she whispered, her eyes filling, and, reaching up, she pulled his head down and kissed him.

He drew away fractionally, just enough to speak. 'Do you want me to use a condom?'

She reached for him again. 'No—no, it isn't necessary. Just make love to me, please—now. . .'

He moved over her, his control shattering, and she felt him fill her as she had never been filled.

'Oh, Charlotte, that feels so good,' he groaned.

Her eyes welled with tears, and her legs wrapped round him, drawing him even closer to her heart.

'Keep still,' he gritted, but she couldn't. Ripples of sensation were starting deep inside her and she was helpless to resist.

'I can't,' she whispered, and with a ragged groan he started to move, his body pounding into hers until the ripples turned to a tidal wave and broke over her. She clung to him, crying his name, and felt the savage shudders of his release and the hot, pulsing flood of his essence spilling deep within her.

She clung to him, her hands pressed hard against the

sweat-slicked skin of his back, revelling in the welcome weight of his body. For an age he was silent, then he lifted his head and looked at her as if he had just discovered a miracle.

'Are you OK?' he murmured.

She nodded, beyond coherent speech, and he hugged her gently before shifting his weight to the side and drawing her into his arms. 'Go to sleep,' he mumbled, and seconds later his even breathing told her he had done just that.

With a contented sigh she joined him.

She woke to the sensation of drifting on a sea of musk-scented roses. For a moment she lay still, groping for memory, and then he shifted beside her and everything came back, every last touch, every sigh, every kiss.

The air was much cooler now, the draught from the window chilling her flesh, but they were lying on the quilt and she didn't want to wake him.

He grunted and turned towards her, sighing deeply as he pulled her into his arms.

'You're cold,' he mumbled.

'Mmm.'

He roused himself enough to tug the quilt out from underneath them and snuggle them both down in its warm embrace, then, curling round her so that they lay like spoons in a drawer, he wrapped his arm over her waist and made a deep, contented noise in the back of his throat.

Seconds later he was asleep again.

She lay in his arms, his chest warm and solid behind her back, and allowed herself to float between sleep and wakefulness, relishing the moment.

He woke shortly before eleven, hungry and thirsty,

and raided the kitchen, bringing some dips and crisps
back to bed. They drank fizzy mineral water and fed
each other crisps coated with taramasalata and
hummus, then he put the tray on the chest of drawers
and advanced on her.

The light was still on, and his intention was quite
clear. Charlotte found the mere sight of him was
enough to arouse her, and she welcomed him with
open arms. Their union was swift and shattering in its
intensity, and afterwards she cried.

'What is it?' he asked softly. 'Did I hurt you?'

She shook her head. 'No—no, you could never hurt
me. I'm being silly. It was just so beautiful.'

He hugged her close, raining tender kisses on
her face, and then he tucked her into his side and
they slept again, waking to the birds greeting the
dawn.

She groaned and turned over, but he chased her,
his lips nibbling over her shoulder, and she turned
back to him.

'Good morning,' he whispered.

'Morning.'

'You look beautiful.'

She laughed, a small, satisfied sound. 'So do you—
dark and dishevelled and mysterious and very,
very sexy.'

'Mmm—very sexy. I want you again,' he told her.

'Then have me,' she said simply.

'There isn't time.'

'There is for you.'

'No—no, Charlotte, not like that.'

She smoothed his face. 'Why not? Not all the time,
but sometimes, why not? You make me so mindless I
can't concentrate on you—I want to watch you, just

this once—anyway,' she said with a shy smile, 'I owe you.'

'You owe me nothing,' he protested.

'Please?'

He stared into her eyes for a long time, fighting with his instincts, and then she saw him buckle and surrender.

'I can't resist you,' he said, his voice ragged, and, easing over her, he entered her slowly, carefully, giving her time to adjust.

'That feels so good,' he said through gritted teeth, and, lowering his mouth to hers, he kissed her deeply as he began to move, mimicking his penetration.

Her hands smoothed over his back, revelling in the supple shift of muscle under his hot, satin skin, and as she dragged her nails lightly down his spine he groaned and lifted his head.

'God, woman,' he breathed, and she watched, entranced, as he began to thrust deeply into her.

His face grew taut, the cheekbones flushed dark with desire, and as his skin grew slick beneath her palms so he shuddered, his head thrown back, a hoarse cry on his lips.

Her own climax followed seconds later and left her stunned and shaking.

'Charlotte?' he murmured, and she turned her head into the hollow of his shoulder and placed a tender kiss against his skin.

'I love you,' she mouthed, and his arms tightened, almost as if he had heard her.

He eased away from her and smoothed her hair back from her face, gazing down at her with an expression of such tenderness that her eyes welled.

'Oh, sweetheart,' he said gently, and, folding her

back into his arms, he cradled her lovingly against his chest. 'So much for leaving you behind,' he said with an affectionate chuckle.

'It was your fault,' she told him. 'It was watching you—you looked so——' Words failed her, and she hugged him hard.

He laughed softly, his breath teasing her hair, and then he swung away from her, bounding off the bed and stretching luxuriously.

'Last one in the shower's a rotten egg,' he threw over his shoulder, and she chased him, giggling, into the bathroom.

As the weeks passed, so her love for him grew, fuelled by his tenderness, his humour and his almost infinite sensitivity, not only to her but to the mothers in his care.

A fortnight after the start of their affair a young woman was admitted, accompanied by her partner and another woman, a friend who she asked to be allowed to stay with them.

'She does shiatsu, and I'm very frightened. I want her with me,' the girl, Pru, told them.

Bev Linari was on duty and Pru's partner, Nick, asked if he could have a word with her and with the doctor on duty.

It happened to be Charlotte, so they went into the sister's office.

'She's got problems,' he told them. 'She was abused by her stepfather when she was a child, and it's taken years to deal with it. She's really scared that this experience will bring it all back, and she's terrified about having control taken away from her.'

'That's OK,' Bev said. 'If everything goes well, she

won't need any medical intervention at all, and if it doesn't, then we can make sure she still feels in control. Dr Jennings here will be on duty for the rest of the day, and Mr Parry, the senior registrar, is very gentle and sympathetic. He's a great believer in natural child-birth, so you won't find any opposition from him.'

Nick shifted awkwardly. 'It's just that we've heard things about the consultant—that he's a bit of a butcher, you know?'

Bev's loyalty was clearly torn. In the end she compromised. 'He's an excellent surgeon,' she assured him, 'and if surgery should be necessary she couldn't be in better hands. However, the chances of getting the great man himself to attend to you are very slight, so she's probably safe!'

Nick nodded, a fleeting smile touching his face. 'Good. Can she walk round? Use the water pool?'

'Oh, yes. We've also got a TENS machine, short for Transcutaneous Electrical Nerve Stimulation, and she can use that to help with the pain relief. It works by triggering our own natural production of endorphins and enkephalins which help us to deal with the pain, and by reducing the transmission of pain signals to the brain.'

'Yes, we've heard about it but it's got wires, hasn't it? So she can't walk around.'

'Oh, she can to a certain extent, but of course you can't use it in the water pool, and it makes back mass-age difficult.'

'Who's the friend?' Charlotte asked.

'Oh, Mel, she does shiatsu—like reflexology but all over the body. She's got some oils and things, and teas—can she use them?'

'Yes, of course,' Bev assured him. 'In fact we have

most of the commonly used aromatherapy oils like lavender and jasmine in the delivery suite anyway.'

'Oh—right.' He looked a little happier at that, and, having laid his fears to rest, Bev went to check on Pru.

'It might be an idea if she gets to know you, too, so that if she needs any medical attention she's already met you,' Bev said to Charlotte.

So they went in together, and Pru was visibly relieved that there was a woman doctor in attendance. 'I don't want a man touching me,' she said unsteadily. 'This whole thing is going to be difficult enough without that—and I want Nick and Mel with me for the whole thing, no matter what.'

Charlotte smiled sympathetically. 'Don't worry, they'll be here. And remember, we all want it to be simple and pain-free, as much as you do. I gather Mel's going to be massaging you and using shiatsu—would you mind if I see how she does it? I find it fascinating.'

'No, of course—that's fine. Can I call you Charlotte?'

Charlotte smiled. 'Sure. Look, I have to go and help with a clinic for a while, Pru, but I'll pop back every now and then, and maybe when things get a bit closer I can find a bit more time to be in here. OK?'

In fact Charlotte had plenty of time after the clinic before things hotted up with Pru's labour. William was in Theatre and she was doing rounds of gynae post-ops when she was paged.

Bev thought she might want to come and see the shiatsu massage in progress, and also reacquaint herself with Pru who was doing really well.

'She's gained so much confidence during the day, but I've got a bad feeling,' Bev said quietly while Nick and Mel were massaging Pru through a contraction.

She was in the water pool, looking calm and in control, and Charlotte could see nothing wrong.

However, she trusted Bev's instincts. 'Any idea why?'

She shook her head. 'No. Presentation seems good—maybe it'll be a big baby, or a stargazer. I can't tell till the cervix dilates a bit more.'

A 'stargazer' was a baby born face first, sometimes in the posterior position, and it resulted inevitably in a protracted second stage, often with a ventouse or forceps delivery.

The problem was that Charlotte was on duty that night, with Derek Blythe on take as back-up, and he was the very last person Pru needed to see. So she decided to have a word with William, just to be on the safe side.

He came down from Theatre an hour later, while Pru was still contracting happily in the pool in the soothing scent of jasmine and lavender. Charlotte made him a cup of tea and told him about Pru's fears and Bev's bad feeling.

'Oh, hell's teeth,' he muttered. 'Well, I'll hang around. I just hope the old man doesn't get called in for anything else and drift past, or he'll get the tongs out.'

'There may be nothing wrong.'

He shook his head. 'If Bev's got a feeling, she's got a feeling. She's been a midwife a hell of a long time, Charlotte. She knows what she's doing.'

Somehow Charlotte didn't find that comforting. All through the night she kept an eye on the situation, and at three a.m. Bev drew her to one side.

'That baby's making heavy weather. I thought it was a stargazer but it's not. There's something else—

probably a shoulder dystocia. If so it'll wedge across the pelvic outlet as the head's delivered. We'll find out soon, but I've got her out of the water.'

Pru looked exhausted, and so did Nick. Only Mel, massaging constantly with jasmine and lavender to soothe and relax, was still intent, her face calm. She was working on the pressure-point in the web between her thumbs and forefingers. 'It's called the Great Reliever,' she told them.

'Talking of which, I need a pee,' Pru said wearily.

Nick took her into the bathroom but she couldn't manage to do anything, and Bev thought she needed catheterising. She explained what she was going to do, and got Pru to lie on her back. Naturally she felt very vulnerable, but Bev talked gently to her the whole time and the entire procedure took only a couple of minutes.

'Oh, that's wonderful,' she sighed as her over-full bladder was able to drain.

Bev carefully removed the catheter and then checked to see if the baby had progressed.

'Oh, yes, it's down further now. I expect that was causing a bit of a hold-up.'

With the obstruction of her bladder out of the way, Pru then began to push, and they helped her up into a squatting position. Moments later the baby's head was delivered, but then with the next contraction there was no progress.

'I think we need William,' Bev told her quietly. 'I'll explain what's happening—could you get him?'

Charlotte went into the little room where the duty doctor was supposed to spend the night. William was stretched out on the bed fully dressed, and she woke him with a kiss.

'Mmm—it's my princess,' he said with a smile. 'Am I going to turn into a frog?'

'Who says you haven't already?' she retorted with a cheeky grin. 'Look, it's Pru—Bev says it might be a shoulder dystocia.'

'Oh, great. Well, lock the doors, because if there's one thing in particular that freaks the old man it's shoulder dystocias. Litigation again. Brachial plexus palsy, fractured humerus and clavicle, late sections, neonatal death—just keep him out. Seduce him or something.'

Her eyes widened, and he hugged her. 'I'm joking. You're mine.'

They went into the delivery-room to find that Bev had tried and failed to deliver the anterior shoulder by gentle traction. Pru was getting panicky, and at the first sight of William she shrank back up the bed.

'No—go away. I don't want forceps,' she sobbed.

William went and stood by her head, so that she didn't fear any immediate intervention, and took her hand. 'Pru, listen—can I call you Pru?'

She turned away. 'Please—don't do it.'

'I don't intend to,' he told her. 'Please listen. Are you listening to me? This is very important.'

After a moment she nodded.

'Your baby's stuck because the shoulders are wide and wedged across the pelvic outlet. It's called a shoulder dystocia, and it's quite tricky. You can't just pull the baby out, or do an episiotomy, or any of the other things that you're afraid of. But what we must do is change your position. Can I show you something? I won't touch you.'

She turned towards him, her eyes fearful.

PLAY ★★★★★★
★★★★★★ **£600,000 LOTTO!**

★★★★★★★★★★★★★★★★★★★★★

NO COST... NO OBLIGATION...

██████████████████████

NO PURCHASE NECESSARY!

IT'S FUN

IT'S FREE

FREE BOOKS! CASH PRIZES!

FREE!
This fluffy duck with the compliments of Mills & Boon.

OFFICIAL RULES
NO PURCHASE NECESSARY TO ENTER
MILLION DOLLAR SWEEPSTAKES (III)

To enter, follow the directions published. Method of entry may vary. For eligibility, entries must be received no later than March 31, 1996. No liability is assumed for printing errors, lost, late or misdirected entries.

To determine winners, the sweepstakes numbers on submitted entries will be compared against a list of randomly, pre-selected prizewinning numbers. In the event all prizes are not claimed via the return of prizewinning numbers, random drawings will be held from among all other entries received to award unclaimed prizes.

Prizewinners will be determined no later than June 30, 1996. Selection of winning numbers and random drawings are under the supervision of D. L. Blair, Inc., an independent judging organisation whose decisions are final. Limit: one prize to a family or organisation. No substitution will be made for any prize, except as offered. Taxes and duties on all prizes are the sole responsibility of winners. Winners will be notified by mail. Odds of winning are determined by the number of eligible entries distributed and received.

Sweepstakes open to residents of the U.S. (except Puerto Rico), Canada, Europe and Taiwan who are 18 years of age or older, except employees and immediate family members of Torstar Corp., D.L. Blair, Inc., their affiliates, subsidiaries, and all other agencies, entities, and persons connected with the use, marketing or conduct of this sweepstakes. All applicable laws and regulations apply. Sweepstakes offer void wherever prohibited by law. Any litigation within the province of Quebec respecting the conduct and awarding of a prize in this sweepstakes must be submitted to the Regies des Loteries et Courses du Quebec. In order to win a prize, residents of Canada will be required to answer a time-limited arithmetical skill-testing question to be administered by mail.

Winners of major prizes (Grand through Fourth) will be obligated to sign and return an affidavit of Eligibility and Release of Liability within 30 days of notification. In the event of non-compliance within this time period or if a prize is returned as undeliverable, D.L. Blair, Inc. may at its sole discretion, award that prize to an alternate winner. By acceptance of their prize, winners consent to use of their names, photographs or other likeness for purposes of advertising, trade and promotion on behalf of Torstar Corp., its affiliates and subsidiaries, without further compensation unless prohibited by law. Torstar Corp. and D.L. Blair, Inc., their affiliates and subsidiaries not responsible for errors in printing of sweepstakes and prize winning numbers. In the event a duplication of a prize winning number occurs, a random drawing will be held from among all entries received with that prize winning number to award that prize.

This sweepstakes is presented by Torstar Corp., their subsidiaries, and affiliates in conjunction with book, merchandise and/or product offerings. •The number of prizes to be awarded and their value are as follows: Grand Prize - $1,000,000 (payable at $33,333,33 a year for 30 years): First Prize - $50,000; Second Prize - $10,000; Third Prize - $5,000; 3 Fourth Prizes - $1,000 each; 10 Fifth Prizes - $250 each; 1000 Sixth Prizes - $100 each. Values of all prizes are in U.S. currency. Prizes in each level will be presented in different creative executions, including various currencies, vehicles, merchandise and travel. Any presentation of a prize level in a currency other than U.S. currency represents an approximate equivalent to the U.S. currency prize for that level, at that time. Prize winners will have the opportunity of selecting a prize offered for that level; however, the actual non U.S. currency equivalent prize, if offered and selected, shall be awarded at the exchange rate existing at 3:00 P.M. New York time on March 31, 1996. A travel prize option, if offered and selected by the winner, must be completed within 12 months of selection and is subject to: travelling companion (s) completing and returning of a Release of Liability prior to travel; and hotel and flight accommodations availability. For current list of all prize options offered within prize levels, send a self-addressed, stamped envelope (WA residents need not affix postage) to MILLION DOLLAR SWEEPSTAKES (III) Prize Options, Reader Service, PO Box 70, Croydon, Surrey, CR9 3JG.

For a list of prizewinners (available after July 31, 1996) send a separate, stamped, self-addressed envelope to: Million Dollar Sweepstakes (III) Winners, Reader Service, PO Box 70, Croydon, Surrey, CR9 3JG.

•U.K. equivalent prize values at the time of printing. Grand Prize - £600,000; First Prize - £30,000; Second Prize - £6,000; Third Prize - £3,000; 3 Fourth Prizes - £600 each; 10 Fifth Prizes - £150 each; 1,000 Sixth Prizes - £60 each.

Mills & Boon invite you to play

£600,000 LOTTO!

LOTTO CARD No: PW289920

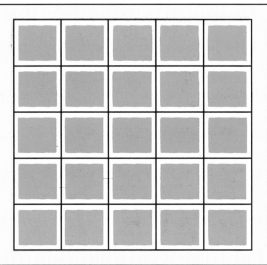

LOTTO SQUARES SCRATCH OFF

Instructions: Using a coin, scratch away silver squares, in a straight line (across, down or diagonal) until 5 hearts are revealed. Doing this makes you eligible for a chance to win one of the following prizes: Grand Prize, £600,000; First prize £30,000; Second Prize £6,000; Third Prize £3,000; Fourth Prize £600. VOID IF MORE THAN 5 SILVER SQUARES ARE SCRATCHED AWAY.

AND... YOU CAN CLAIM UP TO 4 FREE LOVE ON CALL NOVELS A FLUFFY DUCK AND A MYSTERY GIFT ABSOLUTELY FREE.

To register your entry in the £600,000 Prize Draw and to claim your free books and gifts simply return this card. See the coupon overleaf.

We are sure that once you have read your free books, you'll want more of the heartwarming romances. So unless we hear otherwise, every month we will send you 4 of our very latest Love on Call novels for just £1.80* each. Postage and packing are free - we pay all the extras! Your satisfaction is guaranteed! You may cancel or suspend your subscription at any time, simply by writing to us. Any free books and gifts will remain yours to keep.

*Prices subject to change without notice.

DON'T HESITATE REPLY TODAY!

FREE BOOKS CERTIFICATE

YES! Please send me the free books and gifts to which I am entitled and enter me in the £600,000 Prize Draw. Please also reserve a Reader Service subscription for me. I understand that I am under no obligation, as explained overleaf, and that I may cancel at anytime simply by writing to you.

If you would like to enter the £600,000 prize draw but would prefer not to receive books please tick box. ☐

Ms / Mrs / Miss / Mr _____

Address _____

_____

_____

_____ Postcode _____

2A5D

MILLS & BOON READER SERVICE
FREEPOST
P.O. BOX 70
CROYDON
SURREY
CR9 9EL

NO
STAMP
NEEDED

'See my hands.' He made a ring with his fingers and thumbs, and pressed down on to the bed so that the ring flattened. 'This is what happens when you lie on your back. Now, if we get you up, like this, on to all fours, this is what happens.' He stretched his fingers, widening the circle and gapping slightly with the thumbs.

'You have ligaments that can give, and you can add perhaps thirty per cent to that diameter of the pelvis by getting into that position. Often that's enough. If that doesn't work, then usually by carefully persuading the arm against your backbone to come round the baby can be delivered quite happily without any further intervention. But we can't do this; you have to do it yourself. It's in your control. We can help, but *you* have to do it.'

That seemed to be the turning point. Pru agreed reluctantly, and William quickly washed and tugged on a pair of gloves. Just then she had another contraction, and the baby's face screwed up and it cried out, a little mewling sound.

William winced. 'Come on, Pru, let's get you up— that baby's being squashed now.'

With William on one side and Nick on the other, they lifted her up and helped her on to all fours.

William checked the position, and shook his head. 'It looks better, but it's still stuck. I'm going to slide my fingers round behind the baby's shoulder and see if I can help to widen that opening a little more, OK? Are you ready, Pru? I'll try not to hurt you, but I may not be able to help it. I'll be as gentle as I can.'

Pru moaned and leant against Nick, and Charlotte watched tensely as William carefully worked his fingers round behind the baby's head and in over the shoulder.

Then she saw the muscles in his arm bunch and he lifted up against the sacrum.

With a slithering splosh, the baby literally shot out into Bev's waiting hands.

She grinned at Charlotte. 'That's another of his party tricks.'

Charlotte felt stunned. While Bev held the baby, William and Nick helped Pru to lie down again and then Bev placed the perfectly healthy little boy in her arms.

'Oh, thank God it's not a girl,' she said with a sob, and wrapped her arms around her son, cradling him protectively, her labour forgotten for now in the sheer relief of holding her baby safely in her arms.

William's eyes were stormy, and she knew he was furious with the man that had taken Pru's confidence in herself as a woman and ground it into dust.

He squeezed her shoulder in congratulation, praised the way she had coped with a very difficult delivery and then left.

'He's gone,' Pru said a minute later. 'I wanted to thank him.'

'I'll pass it on,' Charlotte told her. 'I think he wanted to get out of your way—he was very conscious of the fact that you didn't really like him being here.'

'I hope I didn't hurt his feelings—I was just so scared about losing control. Do you know, he didn't once make me feel like a piece of meat?'

'He wouldn't,' Charlotte said quietly. 'I feel very privileged to have worked with him. He has a real gift.'

'He certainly has,' Bev said in a quiet aside. 'There isn't anyone else in the hospital who could have done that so slickly, and as for the old man—well! You know he's due to retire at Christmas, do you? I hope

William gets the consultancy. He certainly deserves it.'

'Is he going to apply?' Charlotte asked. 'He hasn't mentioned it.'

Bev grinned slyly. 'I expect you've just distracted him. Nothing like a new affair to end sane conversation.'

Charlotte blushed. 'God, does everybody know?'

Bev laughed. 'Probably not everybody. I doubt if the old man knows.' She looked at Charlotte's face and gave a sympathetic smile. 'Hey, it's OK. Everyone thinks it's great. We're all very fond of William. It's time he found someone else.'

Charlotte felt panic rising inside her. Did they all think it was going to turn into something permanent? She hoped not, and she hoped desperately that William didn't think so.

No, he couldn't. If he did, by now he would have told her that he loved her, and he hadn't.

Wanted, yes, and needed, but loved? No.

Only in her dreams.

CHAPTER SIX

'EVERYONE seems to know about us,' Charlotte told him later the next day.

They were having supper in his conservatory. William had cooked it while she'd curled up on the squashy cushions and slept for a while, and she was feeling a little more refreshed after her hectic day and night. Now, she thought, might be the time to mention the remark Bev had made.

'They do?' He shot her a look. 'Does that worry you?'

She shook her head. 'No, not really, I don't suppose. I just didn't want it to affect your chances of getting the consultancy.'

He paused, fork at his mouth, and put it down again. 'I haven't even decided if I should apply yet,' he told her.

'I think you should.'

'On account of my long fingers?' He wagged them at her and grinned suggestively.

She smiled. 'No. On account of your natural gift for helping women in childbirth.'

He laughed awkwardly, clearly embarrassed by her praise. 'Blythe said I should have been a midwife— he thinks I never learnt where midwives end and doctors begin.'

'The man's a fool,' Charlotte said vehemently. 'Intervention is only justified as a last resort, not to make life easier for the attendants!'

He grinned. 'We'll make an obstetrician of you yet,' he teased.

'No, I don't think so. It's too traumatic.'

'Traumatic?' he exclaimed. 'It's probably the least traumatic branch of medicine—not gynae, of course, but obstetrics, anyway. I mean, think about it. Women get pregnant because they're well and healthy. That makes the care they need different from the care needed in any other branch of medicine. You're helping them do what comes naturally, not helping them carry on despite what's wrong. No, most of the time it's not traumatic at all.'

That depended, Charlotte thought, on your viewpoint, and the trauma she was talking about was her own, not that of the patients. It was all very well if you were married and having your own children, but if you couldn't—if there was some reason that prevented that happy state of affairs, how could you cope? Take Alex and Jo Carter, unable to have children and working all day with pregnant women.

Turning the knife wasn't in it. And for Charlotte, whose dreams of happy ever after had been shattered long ago, having the knife turned on a daily basis was not something she was enjoying.

No, come February she would move on to some other discipline, probably geriatrics, and her battered heart could settle down again.

In the meantime, she had William and her dreams. Maybe that could keep her going.

The next few weeks in the maternity unit were very busy—too busy for mawkish sentiment, Charlotte thought gratefully. William applied for the consultancy, and then sat back to wait.

Fortunately, being busy kept his mind occupied as well, because he was clearly more nervous about it than he was admitting.

Pru and her baby had gone home two days after her somewhat hectic delivery, and she sent William a letter thanking him for his help and apologising for being so anti.

'I should think she had a right to be anti, the way she'd been treated, poor girl,' he said, but Charlotte could tell he was touched.

William wasn't the only one who reacted to the previous ill-treatment of the women in their care. On one occasion when Alex Carter's team was on call, there was a great deal of screeching and kerfuffle, which resulted in several Arab women in black robes being ejected from the ward.

A couple of hours later Jake Hunter appeared in the ward kitchen, shaking from head to foot.

'Any chance of a coffee?' he muttered.

William handed him the one he had just made, and Jake swallowed half of it and then set it down.

'My God,' he said under his breath.

'Problems?' Charlotte asked.

'Problems? I'll say. Have you ever seen a Pharaonic circumcision?'

Charlotte blanched. 'Oh, no.'

'Oh, yes. A Sudanese girl of seventeen, married for a year, having her first baby. Bev called me the second she examined her. The women didn't want me in there, but the girl pleaded for help so I chucked them all out. Her grandmother did it on the kitchen table with scissors when she was seven, she told me. She's got no clitoris, no labia, just a tiny hole to pee through and for her husband to——'

He broke off and downed the rest of the coffee. 'How the hell she got pregnant I can't imagine. The opening was so tiny I could scarcely get two fingers through it. Intercourse must have been agony, and she was supposed to be cut open for the birth and then sewn up again. I can't do it. I can't sew her up that tight, and I won't.'

He stabbed trembling fingers through his hair and looked at William. 'What do we do? What does the law state? Where do we go from here?'

'Has she had the baby?'

He shook his head. 'No, she's in labour now. Bev's with her. She's had an epidural, and I've opened her vulva as well as I can, but she needs major reconstructive surgery, and even that will never give her back her sexuality. Just the semblance of it. God, it makes me weep.'

Charlotte looked at him, and found tears clogging his lashes. Lucky Annie, she thought, with a husband as caring and compassionate as that.

'I'll check the medico-legal situation with the management,' William was saying. 'Meanwhile just give her lots of TLC and hope to God the baby's a boy.'

Jake let out his breath in a long, ragged sigh. 'Yeah, I suppose you're right. Oh, God, I hate things like this. I'm just glad Annie's on maternity leave so she doesn't have to see it.'

'How is Annie?' Charlotte asked.

'Oh, making progress. She's getting tired now—she's nearly there. That's the next thing I'll find to panic about, of course. She said her first labour was awful, and because I wasn't there I don't know what went wrong. I gather it was horribly protracted—you know she wants you to deliver it, do you?' he said to William.

'Oh, God, no—the responsibility,' William groaned. 'How about Alex? At least he's a consultant.'

'You might be before long.'

William grunted. 'Maybe. If they ask the old man's opinion, there's no way I'll get it. Too darned controversial for words. Anyway, how about you? Aren't you applying?'

He shook his head. 'No—I haven't got the relevant experience yet. I spent too long in America and Romania. Maybe the next one to come up.'

'That'll be Julia Carmichael in about ten years. You'll want something before then.'

He shrugged. 'We'll see. I'm not in a hurry. I just want our baby safely born before I find anything else to worry about.' He shrugged away from the worktop and circled his shoulders. 'I'll be in delivery suite two,' he told William. 'Let me know what I have to do about this girl, could you?'

William went into the ward sister's office to try and find out the legal position, and Charlotte went up to Gynae to check some post-op patients. By the time she came down the Islamic girl had given birth to a perfectly healthy boy, and Alex Carter was talking to her and to her husband about how her repair should be tackled.

Jake tracked them down at the end of the day and told them that Alex had taken her to Theatre and repaired her as well as possible, but had not closed the opening of her vulva as before on the request of her and her husband.

'Apparently it was hurting him too, so they agreed it should be made as normal as possible.'

'Normal?' William said with a humourless laugh. 'Poor bloody kid.'

That night, as he made love to Charlotte, touching her intimately with a tender, careful hand, she felt tears well in her eyes.

Poor girl, she thought, that she could never know the joy so many women took for granted. Not herself—she would never take it for granted, not after her bitter and loveless marriage—but so many women did, as they should. It was their birthright, the flower of their womanhood, and she mourned for all the women who had lost it forever.

The next day the plight of the little Islamic girl was forgotten in the general excitement as Lizzi Hamilton went into labour.

Ross was like a cat on hot bricks, and several times during the morning Charlotte saw him diving into the kitchen and gulping cold water.

Lizzi was being induced at thirty-eight weeks and given a trial of labour. The baby was fine for size, but as Lizzi had an android pelvis and had had difficulty with her first it was considered a good idea for her to be induced rather than risk a post-mature baby with a hard head.

Sue Coulter was the midwife who would stay with Lizzi during her labour, as was the practice in the unit, and when she came out for a coffee-break Charlotte asked how it was going.

'Oh, fine. She's in the water pool, having a wonderful time. She says it feels fantastic, and she's drinking jasmine tea and getting Ross to rub her with jasmine and lavender oil, and she's generally doing really well.'

'Ross isn't,' Charlotte said drily, and Sue laughed.

'No, I'd noticed. That's the trouble with medical people—they panic. We had the same thing with

Oliver and Bron Henderson last month.'

'Has she had her baby?' Charlotte asked.

'Oh, yes—had it on the Saturday morning and went home in the afternoon. No problems at all, easiest delivery in the world. She's an old hand, though—it's their third. Two girls and a boy now. I think the boy's a terror and I got the impression she was pleased to have another girl! Oh, well, must get on—I'll go and soothe Ross!'

Charlotte sighed. Two down, two to go, she thought. Only Lizzi Hamilton and Annie Hunter were left, and Lizzi was well under way. They were all William's contemporaries, men and women of a similar age or a little older, their lives all happily on target.

Did William resent them? Did he feel bitter about the loss of his wife and child at a time that should have been so happy? Inevitably, she thought, although he was such a naturally warm and generous person he probably wouldn't resent them as another person might—herself, for instance.

At the end of the ward she heard a baby cry, and a few minutes later Sue came out beaming. 'Little girl, no problems,' she said to Charlotte who was trapped at the nurses' station writing up notes.

Her heart twisted. 'How lovely—give them my congratulations,' she said, and busied herself with the paperwork.

It was the middle of October, and William decided it was time Charlotte started doing some of the surgery herself.

She had already learned how to do quite complicated vaginal repairs following tears or episiotomies, and had closed for William after Caesarian sections, but she had never done a section on her own or used the ventouse or forceps.

Not that she would do it now without his supervision, but when a healthy woman with a singleton pregnancy and a low placenta came in for an elective section under general anaesthetic William decided it would be a good starting-point.

It was an operation Charlotte had seen him perform several times, but she was still nervous and rather uncertain.

'Don't worry, I'll be right beside you,' he told her, 'and because the patient will be unconscious I can talk you through it blow by blow.'

When she picked up the scalpel to make the first incision, her hand trembled and she sighed.

'You'll be fine,' he told her. 'Nice clean, light sweep along the skin crease—that's it, not too deep. Lovely. Right, go back over it, getting deeper every time— that's it. Well done.'

The nurses were doing their job, swabbing, cauterising, keeping the field clear so that she could see, and under William's calm, gentle guidance she managed to open the uterus without any mistakes.

'You lift the baby out, go on,' he said with a smile, and she reached in her hands and coaxed the slippery infant out through the opening she had made in the uterus.

It wriggled and let out a yell, and she laughed in delight. 'I did it,' she said, and her eyes prickled. 'Oh, hell.'

She leant over and wiped her eyes against William's shoulder, and above his mask she saw his eyes crease in a smile.

'Well done. Right, hand the baby over, and let's get

this placenta out and the uterus closed.'

She managed the whole operation without a single error, and for the rest of the day she was in cloud-cuckoo-land.

Maybe obstetrics wouldn't be such a bad field, she thought that night, if she could only concentrate on the job and keep her personal life at a distance.

She concentrated on obstetrics that week, but the following week she expressed an interest in the gynae ops.

'I know it's not that relevant for general practice, but if I changed my mind and switched to obs and gynae I could use some experience.'

So the next time William had a list she took a couple of the cases, but there was one he wouldn't allow her to do.

'I'll take the last case,' he said firmly, and tried to send her out of the operating suite.

'What is it?' she asked.

'A termination. I don't want you to have to do it.'

She swallowed. 'It's part of the job, though, isn't it?'

'Yes. And unfortunately, until we can devise a method of contraception that's totally foolproof, it's going to remain a part of the job. That doesn't mean you have to do it.'

'It seems a dreadful thing to have to do when so many people want babies and can't have them,' she said quietly.

'That doesn't worry me as much as the effect on the mother in years to come, knowing what she's done. Some of them have very real problems in later life—severe depression, guilt, self-hatred. It's easy at the time, but once it's done you have to live with yourself. That's why I always spend a long time with them trying to talk them out of it, and if time isn't running out I try and get them to go and spend a week thinking about it. It's surprising how many come back seven months later and go home delighted with their babies.'

'But not this one.'

His face grew grave. 'No, not this one. Mind you, it's her third termination and, frankly, I know it's a brutal thing to say but the baby may be better off. If she suffered a little guilt, maybe she'd take better care to avoid pregnancy in the first place.'

'Can't you persuade her to be sterilised?' Charlotte asked.

'At seventeen?'

Charlotte was appalled. 'This is her third termination and she's only seventeen? What are her parents thinking about?'

He shrugged. 'Something else, clearly. She's a stroppy little piece of work—I expect she hasn't been a bundle of laughs to bring up herself.'

'Oh, God, what a mortal coil.'

He laughed without humour. 'Ain't it just. Well, are you staying or going?'

She swallowed. 'I'll stay. I should. It's part of the job. You have to take the rough with the smooth.'

So she stayed, and felt sick. She hadn't expected the rough to feel so rough.

William talked her through it later over lunch, while he coaxed her to eat, and gradually she felt a little better, although far from reconciled.

'How do you do it? Do you get used to it?'

'Sort of,' he told her. 'You just have to blank it out. Jake hates it. He was doing hundreds a week in Romania. I think that took some blanking out.'

'I'm sure. When's their baby due?'

'The end of November. About four or five weeks, I think. That's one delivery I'm dreading. Annie was so scared about getting pregnant after her first labour, but she seems to have decided that if I'm about things will be fine. I just hope she isn't in for a rude shock.'

Charlotte gave a little laugh. 'I doubt it. Having seen you in action, I'm quite sure that if anything goes wrong you'll sort it out better than anyone else could.'

He leant towards her, his eyes twinkling. 'Could you be just the teeniest bit biased?' he asked.

'Me?' Her eyes widened innocently. 'Of course not—perish the thought.'

He chuckled. 'Hmm. Oh, by the way, my father's sixty-five this week and we're having a bit of a family party at the weekend. Mum asked if you'd like to join us.'

Her heart thumped. 'Join you?'

'Yes—me, my two sisters, their respective partners and various offspring—nothing drastic, just a quiet celebration. I'm going down on Saturday morning and coming back on Sunday.'

'How do they know about me?' she asked, amazed.

'Because I told them, of course. Well? Will you?'

She lifted her shoulders in an eloquent little shrug.

'Do you think I should? I mean, I'm not part of the family or anything like that.'

'Charlotte, don't be silly,' he said, without elaboration. 'I'll tell her you're coming. OK?'

And so she went with him, somewhat apprehensively, and found herself in the middle of what she could only describe as affectionate chaos.

The house, buried deep in the heart of the New Forest, was large and rambling and seemed full of children.

They were greeted in the hall by cries of delight and much hugging and kissing in which Charlotte found herself included, to her surprise and slight discomfort.

Heavens, they were all so affectionate!

'Charlotte, this is Kate, my sister, her husband Tom, the children—oh, where are they? Here. Molly, Anna and Will. Say hello.'

Six eyes the colour of William's stared up at her. 'Hello,' they mumbled in unison, then turned back to William, clamouring for his attention. He hoisted the little boy up into his arms, ruffled the girls' hair and turned to his other sister.

'Charlotte, meet Lucy and her boyfriend Stephen. Where are the folks?'

'Here.'

He turned at the voice and a warm, loving smile spread over his face.

'Mum, you look wonderful,' he said, and, handing little Will back to his father, he crossed the hall in a stride and swept his mother up into a bear-hug.

'Oh, it's good to see you again,' he said, reaching for his father and including him in the hug.

'Well, we're always here,' his mother said in mock-reproach. 'You've been neglecting us, and I can see why.'

Her smile settled on Charlotte, and William drew her forward. 'Mum, I'd like you to meet Charlotte. Charlotte, my parents, Judith and Michael.'

'Hello, my dear,' Judith said warmly. 'It's good to meet you at last—we've heard so much about you.'

She hugged her briefly, then Charlotte found herself staring up into a pair of twinkling eyes an exact replica of William's. 'Good to see you—thank you for sparing the time to come and join us.'

Michael kissed her lightly on the cheek, and then wrapped his arm round her shoulders and gave her a little hug. 'You're very welcome, my dear,' he said gruffly. 'Very welcome.'

Charlotte felt her eyes fill. So long excluded from any real family life, she suddenly felt overdosed on it.

She turned to William. 'I'll get the things in from the car,' she said a little breathlessly, and turned blindly towards the door.

He followed her out and drew her into his arms.

'Are you OK?'

She nodded. 'It's just all a bit much.'

He laughed softly. 'You'll get used to it. They'll stick a tea-towel in your hand shortly and you'll just be part of the family.'

Her heart contracted. That was the trouble, of course. She could never be part of the family.

She picked up her suitcase and tugged it out of the boot of his car.

'Here, let me.'

'I'm not paralysed. If you'll just tell me where my room is, I'll go and hang up my dress.'

He shrugged and pulled the other case from the car.

'Fair enough. Come on, then.'

They found his mother in the kitchen. 'We're just going to unpack,' he told her. 'Where have you put us?'

'In your room,' she said, peering into the oven. 'Oh, dear, I hope this casserole's going to be done in time. It did say long and slow, but. . .'

Charlotte turned to William and stared blankly at him.

'Together?' she mouthed.

He shrugged and led her out of the kitchen and up the stairs, to a big room at the back overlooking the garden. The bed, a high, old-fashioned bed with carved mahogany ends, sat squarely against the wall opposite the windows. Both sides were turned down, and there were flowers on the dressing-table.

'Together,' he said, and grinned. 'Oh, well, it'll save us sneaking around.'

Charlotte felt her face flood with embarrassment.

'But they're your parents,' she said, appalled.

'So? How do you think I got here—by stork? Anyway, they know we're as good as living together.'

Charlotte shut her eyes and plonked down on the edge of the bed.

'They must have another bedroom,' she said unhappily.

'I doubt it. Kate and Tom will be in Kate's room, the baby will be in the dressing-room off it, the girls will be in the little room opposite and Lucy and Stephen will be in Lucy's room. That's it—apart from the attic, which is full of spiders, and I don't intend to sleep there for anyone.'

'I want to see it,' she said firmly.

'No,' he said just as firmly. 'Charlotte, you're being ridiculous. If you make a fuss Mum will get all upset and embarrassed, and start moving people round and sleeping in the study and God only knows what. Please, for everybody's sake, just play along. After all, it isn't as if we aren't lovers.'

She swallowed, her anger draining. Another thought had occurred to her.

'Did you sleep here with Eleanor?' she asked.

The bed dipped beside her and his arm came round her shoulders, holding her against his side.

'Yes, I did,' he said quietly. 'Many times.'

A tiny shudder ran through her, and he gave a short

sigh and stabbed his fingers through his hair.

'Charlotte, I'm not going to pretend she didn't exist. She did, and I loved her, and she was a very important part of my life. But that part is over, and lying in this bed with you won't be disloyal either to her or to you. I don't think of her when I hold you, or when I make love to you, or afterwards, when we're lying together in the dark. If there's a spectre in our bed it's that bastard who married you and made your life such a misery. At least I know what love can mean.'

He turned her towards him, his hands on her shoulders. 'Charlotte, listen to me,' he said seriously. 'Eleanor's dead. She's no threat to you.'

Charlotte felt the sob welling up and sagged against him. 'I'm sorry,' she whispered. 'I just don't belong here. They're all looking at me and weighing me up and considering me, as if I've come to take Eleanor's place, and I feel such a fraud!'

His arms closed round her, rocking her gently against his chest. 'Oh, love, I'm sorry. They're just curious— I haven't brought anyone home since Eleanor died, and I suppose they're all letting their imaginations run away with them. I'll tell them——'

'What? That we're just having a casual relationship? Then they'll think I'm a slag.'

He laughed and hugged her. 'No, they won't. Anyway, it isn't a casual relationship, at least not for me. You mean a lot to me, Charlotte. You realise that, don't you? I've had a couple of affairs in the last few years, but nothing that meant anything—nothing that made me think of the future. But now——' she felt his shoulders move in a little shrug '—who knows? Maybe we've got something more, something precious. We'll have to give it time, but meanwhile I'll tell them all to back off and leave you alone. OK?'

She nodded, and he stood up and moved towards the door. She followed him, resting a hand lightly on his arm.

'William?' He stopped and turned back to her. 'Don't make a fuss. I'll be OK.'

'Thank you.' He bent his head and kissed her lingeringly. 'That's till later. I'll go and make some tea. Come down to the kitchen when you're ready.'

She watched him go, then turned and stared at the bed.

'You're safe, Eleanor,' she said quietly. 'I can't have him anyway.'

She went over to the dressing-table, and fingered the sweetly scented roses in the vase. If only. . .

Kate, the older of William's two sisters, was nearly thirty and a vet. Her husband Tom, also a vet, was tall and thin, and said very little except to the children, with whom he was wonderful. Kate clearly adored him, and so did the rest of the family.

Lucy, the youngest of the three Parry offspring, was with her current boyfriend, a medical student like herself. Knowing they weren't married either made Charlotte feel better about sharing a room with William, and rather diffused the situation.

Or perhaps it was William's quiet word that had done that.

Certainly William's parents were very careful what they said to her, and Charlotte hoped he hadn't upset them, because they were possibly the nicest people she had ever met.

His mother Judith, tall, slim, with William's colouring but hazel eyes, was hopelessly disorganised and

delightfully vague, and Michael, quite unmistakably
William's father from the startling blue eyes down-
wards, was quietly efficient, helping with the meal that
evening, his eyes never leaving his wife. He was clearly
devoted to her, and to the rest of his family, and
Charlotte realised that William, too, would be like that
with his own family in years to come. Except, of
course, that she wouldn't be there.

She was seated next to Michael for dinner, with
William on her other side, and their likeness to each
other was disconcerting. Even their voices were the
same—deep and rich and expressive. Only Michael's
hair was noticeably different, a shock of silver-white
in contrast to William's almost black.

'You're very alike,' she told him during dinner. 'I
would have recognised you as his father instantly.'

'Even down to the stubborn streak,' Judith said drily.

Charlotte looked at William in mock-amazement.
'Stubborn streak? Have you been hiding something
from me?'

He laughed and hugged her to his side, and as he
released her Charlotte felt six pairs of eyes trained on
her. She turned her attention to her plate, and the
others collected themselves and the conversation
picked up again. Gradually she relaxed a little, but
never completely, and it was only once they were back
in Suffolk and William had dropped her at her flat that
she really let go.

Exhausted, her cheeks aching from holding a polite
smile on her face all weekend, she crawled into bed
and snuggled under the quilt.

They hadn't made love—it had been late when
they'd gone to bed, and, perhaps out of consideration
of her feelings about Eleanor, he hadn't attempted to

touch her, merely kissing her goodnight and holding her in his arms.

She had needed him, though. She needed him now, for as long as she could have him. Not long, though. Just until February when she moved on. Then she would have to end it, for his sake, in case he fell in love with her.

He still hadn't. She was sure of that, because he had as much as said so. He cared, yes, she knew that. But love? No.

Not yet, at least.

Not on his side.

CHAPTER SEVEN

WILLIAM was interviewed for the consultancy post during the first week of November.

He was extremely nervous, and Charlotte found herself in the position of offering him the encouragement and support he had hitherto been giving her.

The interview panel was to consist of Alex Carter and Julia Carmichael, the other two consultants in the department, Andrew Barrett, the consultant paediatrician in charge of SCBU, an anaesthetist who had worked closely with William over the years and an oncologist with whom he would work in connection with any gynae patients with cancer.

Derek Blythe, the outgoing consultant, was not on the panel, to his disgust, and left William in no doubt of his opinion.

'I hope you didn't expect a glowing reference,' he told him baldly in the middle of the ward the morning of the interview. 'I think the only reason you haven't come a cropper before now is sheer blind luck. You take risks, man—risks. I can't condone that.'

'I take no risks, and you know it,' William said quietly.

Blythe harumphed and stalked off, turning as he left the ward to add a parting shot.

'If you get it, it's the last you'll see of me. I won't work for a hospital that can reward such a slap-dash attitude. They owe me leave, and I shall see that I take it.'

'Feel free,' William muttered under his breath, and stabbed his fingers through his hair.

'You're a mess,' Charlotte told him quietly. 'Comb your hair and stop worrying. You'll be fine.'

'I don't know anything about the opposition.'

'Nor do the interviewing panel, but they know you, very well, and they won't be put off by the old man's blusterings. That gives you a heck of an edge. Better the devil you know and all that.'

He snorted. 'Will you cope? You'll have to call on Blythe if you get stuck.'

'I won't get stuck.'

He closed his eyes. 'Wish me luck,' he muttered.

'Break a leg,' she said softly, and, reaching up, she pressed a kiss to his lips, then turned him and pushed him towards the door. He strode quickly up the ward, and, watching him go, she felt her heart bursting with love. 'Oh, God, please, let him get it,' she murmured.

'How touching,' Bev said in her ear.

She jumped. 'Don't do that to me!'

The midwife grinned. 'William gone for his interview?'

Charlotte nodded. 'I've got butterflies for him!'

'He'll be fine. Alex Carter was asking me a lot of questions about him yesterday—what he was like to work with, what I thought of his professional judgement and competence——'

'And you gave him your usual unbiased opinion,' Charlotte teased.

'Of course!' Bev sobered a little. 'Look, I don't want to worry you, but how do you feel about using the ventouse?'

Charlotte closed her eyes. 'Oh, no. What's the problem?'

'Nothing really—I've got a mum who's been in the second stage for some time, and she's not making very much progress. The liquor's stained with meconium and I think I'd feel happier if we gave the baby a bit of help. It's quite well down, so you should get the cup on easily enough. It's just that if we leave it to Blythe he'll give her a massive episiotomy and yank it out with forceps, and she's done so well it would be a real shame.'

Charlotte felt the butterflies in her tummy multiply faster than fruit bats as they walked towards the delivery suite. 'Look, I'll try,' she said to Bev, 'but I can only do my best. I don't want to risk the baby just to spite Derek Blythe.'

Bev looked appalled. 'Heavens, Charlotte, I wouldn't expect you to. If we can't get anywhere inside five minutes with the ventouse, I think we have to call him. I just wanted you to have a go first. He may be a butcher, but he doesn't lose babies.'

Charlotte's confidence increased once she had met and examined the woman. The baby was, as Bev had said, fairly low, slightly below the level of the ischial spines and almost at the point of crowning. The student midwife who was with her said she had made very slight progress, but every time she relaxed the baby slid back up again. However, the woman had tried to squat and found it impossible, and both she and her husband clearly felt happier with her in a conventional position.

Charlotte explained what she was going to do, and then, attaching a silicone cup to the end of the suction tube while Bev put the woman in stirrups, she tried to remember William's instructions.

First she infiltrated the perineal area with lignocaine,

then, with the suction set on low and pinching the sides of the silicone cup together to form a point, she inserted the point down under the perineum and towards the presenting head. Then, releasing the pressure on the cup, she plopped it on to the baby's head.

To her amazement it held, and she quickly ran a finger round the edge of the cup to ensure that there were no maternal tissues trapped in the edge of the cup. Then, turning up the suction, she waited for a contraction and eased up and back, taking over with more pull as the mother's own expulsive effort eased.

As the contraction passed, the baby's head was clearly lower than it had been, and was almost crowning. Charlotte didn't want to be over-optimistic, but she felt a little surge of adrenalin. It was working, she was sure, and she was managing to do it without help.

Another contraction, another long, slow pull up, and as Bev exhorted the woman the head crowned, stretching the perineum and pausing at the point of birth.

'Tiny push, now, the next time,' Bev warned her.

'Just a little push to help Dr Jennings, and then you need to pant while the head's delivered. OK?'

She nodded, and when the contraction came Charlotte looked at Bev for guidance.

'How much pull?' she asked softly.

'Just up—that's it—I'll guard the perineum—pant, Donna, pant—lovely!'

The head emerged, turned and after a few seconds' rest Bev had the rest of the baby safely in her hands. Charlotte turned off the suction, removed the cup and sagged back against the wall.

She'd done it—she'd delivered a baby, all by herself, using the ventouse!

'Look at that—not even a tiny tear. Well done,' Bev said to her, and she felt her chest swell with pride.

'Congratulations,' she said weakly to the woman, and, having checked for herself that there were no tears or abrasions that needed her attention, she stripped off her gloves and went back out into the ward.

Derek Blythe was just striding towards her.

'Ah, Dr Jennings. Just the person. I'm going to have to do a forceps delivery on the patient in there—you could come and see how it's done properly.'

She buried the smile as deep as she could. 'Actually she's had the baby—she'd progressed a bit and so I used the ventouse just to help lift out.'

He tutted. 'She'll have a nasty tear now, unless you had the forethought to do an episiotomy,' he said sternly.

'Actually, she hasn't. She was very lucky.'

'Or you were,' he said, even more cross now. 'Well, thank your lucky stars nothing went wrong, and in future don't exceed your authority. You mustn't do anything you haven't been trained to do.'

'But I have,' she told him.

He snorted. 'By Parry, I suppose. Dr Ventouse himself. He'll come unstuck one day. Too bloody soft for his own good. Oh, well, I suppose it's only to be expected you'll follow his methods, since you're clearly infatuated with the man.'

And with that he stalked off, leaving Charlotte quite unable to contain her smile any longer. This was one story William was going to enjoy thoroughly!

She didn't see him to talk to all day, because he had a gynae list in the afternoon and she was busy with the pre- and post-ops and with an episiotomy repair—one of the unfortunate women whom Blythe had delivered himself.

'It was quite unnecessary to do such a large cut, even for forceps,' Bev said crossly later, and Charlotte agreed. It took her ages to draw the muscles together to her satisfaction, and by the time she finished her back and neck were aching and she was exhausted.

There was a message for her at the ward clerk's desk.

'Come round—I need TLC PDQ.'

She smiled and stuffed the note in her pocket, then, checking that there were no other messages waiting for her, she hung up her white coat, grabbed her bag and keys and headed for the door.

She drove straight to William's house, anxious to hear how he had got on, and found the door on the latch.

He was in the kitchen on the phone, and reached out his arm towards her. She went up on tiptoe and kissed his cheek, and he winked.

'OK, look, I'll ring you again later, Mum. I want to tell Charlotte all about it; she's just come in.'

He said goodbye, put the phone down and wrapped her in his arms.

'Oh, God, that feels good. I've needed a hug all day,' he mumbled into her hair.

'Well, I'm here as instructed, pretty damn quick, to offer succour. How did it go?'

'Awful,' he groaned. 'I don't know what school of torture that lot attended, but they asked the damnedest questions. "How do you see yourself fitting into the hospital heirarchy?" and "Would you say you had a good self-image?" Awful! It was horrendous! Aaagh!' He gave a mock-shudder and grinned at her weakly.

'So how do you think you did?' she asked.

'I have absolutely no idea at all. I might as well have never met any of them; they were like total strangers. It was ghastly.'

He released her and got two mugs out of the cupboard, pouring the tea that had been brewing in the pot.

'So, how did you get on? I gather you had your first solo flight with the ventouse—Bev said you were brilliant.'

She blushed and laughed. 'Heavens, news travels fast! Were you checking up on me?'

He grinned. 'Would I? Actually, I wondered how much autonomy you'd get with old busy-breeches on the loose. You did well to get away with it.'

She snorted. 'I only just made it—he appeared literally two minutes after I took my gloves off!'

William rolled his eyes. 'That was cutting it a bit fine.'

'I didn't cut it at all—not even a graze. It was a masterpiece; you would have been proud of me.'

He hugged her. 'I was—I am. Let's go out for supper—my nerves are too shot to cook, and you look wiped. We'll go to that bistro, OK?'

'Sounds terrific. I need to go home and change first, though.'

He studied her seriously. 'Maybe you ought to move the rest of your stuff in here.'

She looked quickly away. 'I don't think so. It doesn't look good.' It was a feeble excuse, but the best she could come up with at such short notice. Moving in her clothes was just one step away from moving in, and moving in implied commitment, permanence, and all the trappings of marriage. And that she could never have.

He sighed. 'OK, suit yourself. Though why having a few clothes here is any worse than leaving at six o'clock in the morning God only knows.'

They went to her flat, and she changed into a simple jersey dress that suited her slight figure.

Unfortunately it suited her too well. William took one look at her, his eyes darkened and he held out his arms.

'You look fabulous,' he murmured. 'Come here.'

She was wearing the perfume her sister had sent—more judiciously applied than before, but with the same effect. Moments later her dress was on the chair, his shirt and trousers sailing through the air to join it, and they were lying in a wild tangle on the settee.

'You drive me crazy,' he mumbled into her hair. 'God, you smell so good—I want you. I need you—ah, Charlotte. . .'

Their bodies meshed, and his eyes drifted shut with ecstasy. 'Oh, that feels so good,' he murmured.

Charlotte buried her hands in the soft, thick hair at his nape, steadying his head as she returned his wild kiss. Her deeply sensuous nature, so long denied, had found a soul-mate in William and now, under its influence, her body ran riot, stroking and caressing him, her legs locked around him, drawing him deeper and deeper into the boiling maelstrom of need that consumed her.

She felt the ripples of her completion starting, triggering William's own release, and as he shuddered against her she cried out, her words lost in his own victorious cry of triumph.

They ate much later, without bothering to dress and go out, and it was two in the morning before William remembered he had promised to phone his mother back.

The next two weeks were nerve-racking for both of them. Derek Blythe pounced on them both whenever possible, nit-picking and criticising until William was ready to murder him.

For Charlotte, much less confident in herself, it merely served to undermine her faith in her ability to diagnose and proceed accordingly.

As a result, one patient ended up with a forceps delivery when she could quite easily have got away with the ventouse at the most, and although it was an error of degree that probably made little real difference to the outcome for either mother or baby Charlotte felt she had let the mother down. The resulting episi-otomy and repair was more painful in the initial stages than was necessary, and when Charlotte checked on her the following day she apologised for having had to take such radical action.

'Don't worry,' the woman said forgivingly. 'It was the baby I was worried about, and just so long as he's OK that's all that matters.'

Then one evening while they were in the sitting-room of his house listening to music and trying to relax the doorbell rang.

William left the room, and Charlotte heard Alex Carter's voice in the hall.

'No, Charlotte's here, but that doesn't matter,' William was saying. 'Come in.'

Alex followed him into the room, greeted Charlotte with a smile and then turned to William, whose face was fixed and expressionless.

'You'll get a letter in the post tomorrow,' he said,

'but I wanted to tell you personally—you're being offered the consultancy.'

William was holding his breath, and at Alex's words he let it out in a ragged gust. His eyes drifted shut, and a slow, disbelieving smile played on his lips.

Then his eyes opened and he stared at Alex. 'Are you real? You *are* real!' he said, and then he laughed, a joyous sound that brought tears to Charlotte's eyes.

'Congratulations,' Alex said warmly, shaking his hand, and then William turned to Charlotte and she threw herself into his arms.

'I knew you could do it!' she said, and his arms came round her in a bone-cracking hug, his laughter ringing in her ears.

Somewhere in the confusion Alex left, and William phoned his parents, never letting Charlotte away from his side for a moment. She had never seen him so happy and relaxed, and she realised then how tense he had been, and how much the wait had played on his nerves.

The letter came in the post the following morning, and he read it and re-read it over and over again, as if he still didn't quite dare believe it.

'I told you you'd get it,' Charlotte reminded him.

He grinned wryly. 'I never thought I would, not really, and especially not after that interview. Grilled? I felt like a well-done steak!'

'I wonder how the old man will take it?' she said.

He snorted. 'I imagine it will go down like a lead balloon. Still, if he does what he said he would, he'll take all the leave owing to him and we won't see him again.'

'Can he do that?'

William shrugged. 'I don't think they'd try to stop

him. From something Alex let slip in the past I don't think it's been all sunshine and roses for a long while. Secretly I think the hospital's quite glad to get rid of him.'

With one last slightly disbelieving glance at the letter, he folded it and slipped it into his inside pocket. 'We'd better go,' he told her.

'Time to greet your adoring public,' she teased.

'Oh, rubbish. If they want me it's because they know me and nobody likes change.'

'I think you do yourself an injustice,' she said. 'After all, familiarity breeds contempt—look at Blythe.'

'Do I have to?' he asked wryly.

She laughed. 'Probably not, once he hears the news.'

'I should imagine it's all over the place by now—hospitals are extremely efficient grape-vines.'

He was right. The news had travelled through the unit like a tidal wave.

'He's done it!' Bev yelled, and hugged and kissed a bemused William right in the middle of the ward. Julia Carmichael and Alex Carter came and sought him out to congratulate him and welcome him officially to the consultancy team, and William's delight and pride in himself were a joy to behold.

As Charlotte went about her work and heard everyone else's reaction to his promotion, her heart swelled with pride.

'Great news,' everyone was saying. 'Just what the department needs.'

Everyone, that was, except Derek Blythe, who cleared his desk and left the hospital in a towering rage without so much as a backward glance.

He had six weeks left to go, but he was taking it all in leave, they were told.

'He's no great loss,' Alex said. It was the nearest he had come to criticising the man publicly, and Charlotte was surprised that he should do so.

However, it seemed that discontent and concern about Blythe's professional conduct had been deep-seated, and the hospital management committee had been well aware of public opinion, not only about Derek Blythe, but about William as well.

In a quiet moment he told her that Julia Carmichael had sought him out and told him about the opposition.

'It was very stiff, apparently. I gather I only got the post by a short head. The other main contender was older and more experienced.'

'So what shifted the balance?'

'Apparently something Bev Linari said. Alex and Julia trust her judgement, and she said—oh, well, anyway it swayed them.'

'Go on, tell me—what did she say?' Charlotte prodded.

'No—it doesn't matter.'

'I'll ask her.'

'Oh, hell—she said if she ever had a baby she'd want me to deliver it—and then apologised to Alex for not choosing him.'

Charlotte grinned. 'Good old Bev. Anyway, she's got three children, so you're safe.'

'Yes, but Jake and Annie haven't, and I think that was another factor. Jake said he wouldn't let anybody else near her when she was in labour, apart from a midwife.'

'Are you in danger of becoming smug?' Charlotte asked him pointedly.

'Me?' He grinned innocently. 'Of course not. What are you doing tomorrow night?'

'I don't know—tell me.'

'I want to take you out and celebrate. Go and buy a dress. Julia's firm are on take over the weekend. Get something really gorgeous, and we'll go out to dinner at that new Italian floating restaurant on the river.'

'Good lord—it's terribly expensive!'

'I think I can just about afford it,' he said drily. 'Go on, just this once lash out and spoil yourself. Let's make it an evening to remember.'

So she went to town in the morning and looked for dresses. She tried the little shops, then went into a big department store with a whole designer floor. It was the sort of place she usually avoided like the plague, where if you had to ask the price you couldn't afford it, but just this once she thought it would be appropriate to let herself go.

The final act of her dream perhaps, their swansong.

Because, although he had never told her he loved her, she knew William was beginning to feel more and more for her.

She didn't want to hurt him, any more than she wanted to hurt herself. That pain was unavoidable, and had been since the first time he kissed her, but she could get out before William's heart was too involved.

Tonight, though—she would have tonight, and share his happiness, and let him have his moment of glory. And then tomorrow, or the day after, or the following week. . .

God, it was going to hurt.

She sifted aimlessly through the dresses—long ones, short ones, tiny minis with long, trailing overskirts in gauzy silk; nothing suited either her pocket or her figure.

Then she saw it, an elegant dress with a dropped shawl collar, a fitted bodice and full, softly flaring ballerina-length skirt. It was in the same deep pansy-blue as her eyes, and she loved it on sight.

'Oh, madam, that looks wonderful on you,' the assistant gushed, her copious flattery at the ready. 'With your height and that lovely, slender figure——'

'I'll take it,' Charlotte said, cutting her off.

While the woman wrapped the dress in acres of tissue paper and a big box, Charlotte glanced idly round the rest of the floor, her eyes coming to rest on another department.

Bridal wear.

Oh, God.

Her heart lurched. If only she could—if only there were a way that wouldn't just lead to more pain.

She took her dress, thanking the woman absently, and found her feet leading her across the floor.

The dresses were beautiful—some white, some ivory, some pale pink. There were net ones, satin ones, others of pure silk taffeta. They were beaded, embroidered, some deceptively simple, others frantically over the top.

One, a pale ivory shantung with a heavily beaded bodice and pretty sweetheart neckline, caught her eye. The hem was beaded, the skirt falling from a slightly dropped waist to a pretty little duster train at the back. There was a big, soft bow at the back of the waist, and the sleeves were lightly puffed on the shoulder and narrowed to points over the back of the hand. It was dainty, elegant and Charlotte fell in love with it on the spot. She reached out a hand and touched it almost reverently. If only. . .

'Can I help you, dear?'

She jumped, and the motherly assistant smiled and laid a hand on her arm. 'I'm sorry, I didn't mean to startle you. Do you need any help?'

'Oh—I was just looking at this lovely dress.'

'It is beautiful, isn't it? You suit that slightly dropped waist. I saw you a moment ago in the dark blue dress over there—did you buy it?'

Charlotte smiled. 'Yes, I did. It's for a special occasion.'

'I hope he's worth it.'

Charlotte's heart swelled with pride. 'Oh, he is. Actually, that's the celebration. He's just been made a consultant. He's a doctor at the Audley.'

'Oh, well, it's clearly justified, isn't it? Is he someone special?'

Charlotte looked at the wedding-dress. 'Yes—yes, he is—very special.'

'And have you set a date yet?'

'Date?' She looked at the woman's expectant face, and realisation dawned. In a curious way she almost felt she would be cheating her if she told the truth. And anyway, it wouldn't hurt anyone to play along, just this once. She could dream, couldn't she?

'No,' she said finally. 'We haven't—not yet. Maybe we will tonight. Then I could come back and try it on.'

'I could put it on one side for you till you made up your mind. It's a model, you see—I can't repeat it, and I'd hate you to lose it.'

Charlotte took a deep breath, then smiled at the woman. 'Could I try it?'

The woman's smile lit her face. 'Of course—come on, I'll give you a hand. You'll need the right sort of underwear on, of course, because of the cut of the bodice—what size are you? Thirty-four?'

'Thirty-four A,' Charlotte told her, and with a nod the woman rummaged through a drawer and came up with a lovely lacy strapless bra.

'This will do just to get the effect. Right.'

Minutes later Charlotte found herself standing in front of the mirror while the assistant eased up the concealed zip.

'Oh, what a perfect fit! It could have been made for you. Turn round—oh, my dear, you look lovely!'

She led a bemused Charlotte out on to the shop floor and made her do a twirl in front of the many mirrors arranged around the area.

She could see the front, the back, the sides—she was handed a silk bouquet, a veil on a simple pearl band was placed on her head and the effect was complete.

'Oh, you look beautiful—how lovely!'

Charlotte was speechless. The dress fitted like a dream, but it was more than the fit. It was the way the cream silk made her skin glow, the way the dress emphasised her tiny waist and made the most of her slight breasts. She turned this way and that, stunned at the effect the dress had on her, and then she smiled.

Suddenly she looked radiant, as if she were indeed about to walk down the aisle to William, waiting for her, his love shining in his eyes.

Her lids drifted down, shutting out the image, but it was in her head, in her heart, carved deep into her soul.

'I'm sorry,' she said to the bemused assistant. 'I really don't feel very well. Could you help me change?'

The woman fussed and clucked, worrying over her and offering to call her a taxi as she removed the dress and helped Charlotte into her own clothes.

'I'll be fine—I'm sorry,' Charlotte said, hurrying towards the lift.

'Shall I put it to one side for you?' she called.

Charlotte couldn't answer. Her teeth were clamped firmly on her lip, holding down the sobs that were threatening to choke her.

Dreams, it seemed, were dangerous, more dangerous than she had realised.

Especially when they crumbled into dust.

CHAPTER EIGHT

CHARLOTTE dressed for the meal that night with little enthusiasm. The dress which had seemed so special in the shop now felt like a stage costume, something to wear to assume a part she wasn't qualified to take.

But she had to, for William's sake. This was his night, and for him she had to make it special.

So she wore the dress, and prettied up her hair with a silk flower pinned high up over one ear, and just because it might be the last time she wore the perfume, just the lightest touch on her pulse-points at wrist and throat.

When the bell rang her heart raced, but she steadied herself with a few breaths, dredged up a brave smile and threw open the door.

He took her breath away.

Tall, dark, the sparkling white shirt in dynamic contrast to the immaculate black dinner-suit—he looked spectacular, and she wanted nothing more than to throw herself in his arms and cry her eyes out.

Instead she smiled, twirled and flirted.

'What do you think?'

He shook his head in mute admiration. 'Oh, Charlotte,' he managed eventually, and, reaching out, he pulled her into his arms.

'Uh-uh—I've done my make-up!'

He laughed. 'Tough,' he muttered, just as his lips connected with hers.

It was a searing, heart-racing kiss, and when

he let her go her legs threatened to buckle.

'Oh,' she said softly, and he smiled, a lazy, predatory smile.

'Go and fix your lipstick—we've got a table waiting.'

It was a wonderful meal, course after course of delicate flavours and textures, elegantly presented with the most wonderful service.

It might as well have been sawdust.

Try as she might, Charlotte found it hard to relax and enjoy herself, but she had the feeling she wasn't alone.

William, too, seemed tense for some reason, and when he suggested they forgo the coffee and go back to his house she was more than ready to agree. Frankly, the sooner the evening was over the better.

He put the kettle on, then quickly laid a tray with cups and saucers and cream.

'That looks a bit elegant,' Charlotte commented.

He laughed a little uneasily. 'Mugs seemed rather crude after that exquisite presentation.'

'It was, wasn't it? Thank you for taking me there.'

'Did you enjoy it?'

'Oh, yes,' she lied. 'Why, didn't you?'

He shrugged. 'The food was good. Ignore me, I'm a bit uptight. Come on, the coffee's ready now; let's go through to the sitting-room.'

He flicked on a couple of table-lamps but left the main lights off, creating an intimate and cosy atmosphere.

She headed for a chair, but he cut her off.

'Come and sit on the settee with me.'

There was no way round it without causing a fuss, so she went, curling up in the corner with her feet towards him. He sat at the other end, his legs stretched out and crossed at the ankle, one hand toying absently with her feet.

They drank their coffee in a burgeoning silence, then he put his cup down with a little rattle and turned towards her, hitching one knee up on to the settee so that he was facing her.

'There's something I want to ask you,' he said, and she could see a pulse beating in the hollow of his throat. However, he didn't speak right away, and she waited, puzzled, while he undid his bow-tie and struggled with his top button. Then he braced his hands on his thighs as if to steady them, and, taking a breath, he looked up at her.

'When Eleanor died,' he began, his voice soft and gravelly, 'I thought my life was over. My career went to pieces, my personal life was a wreck—I was devastated. Slowly, bit by bit, I rebuilt my world, a brick here, another brick there. I got my career back on track, bought this house and turned it into a home, but still there was something missing.

'I bought the house deliberately, with the intention of eventually finding a woman I wanted to marry and have children with. I never thought I'd love again— that was too much to ask—but I was fairly sure I could find someone I could be happy with. That was all I asked.'

His breath eased out in a ragged gust.

'Then I met you, and all my preconceived notions flew out of the window because I did something I thought I would never do again—I fell in love.'

Charlotte felt her eyes fill with tears. 'Oh, William,' she whispered.

'I love you, Charlotte. I never thought I'd be able to say that, but I can. I do.'

He took a steadying breath. 'Charlotte, will you marry me? Share my life, my children, my future?'

The tears welled over, splashing on to her dress and making rivers on her cheeks.

'I can't,' she breathed. 'Oh, William, please, don't ask me that!'

She couldn't see his face through her tears, but he moved, taking her in his arms, lifting her so that she lay against his chest.

'Charlotte? Darling, what is it? Why are you crying? You don't have to cry—if you don't love me I'll understand.'

She bit back the tears. She ached to tell him the truth, to say how much she loved him, but she couldn't. He was too much of a gentleman, too generous, too kind. He would do the decent thing and to hell with his own personal happiness. She couldn't do that to him.

So she lied.

'I can't bear to hurt you,' she told him, 'but I don't love you enough—not enough to marry you, anyway. I've been there, William. I know about marriage. Please, don't ask it of me. I can never love you enough for that.'

'Is this all because of Greg?' he said softly. 'Darling, I'm not like him. Your life with me wouldn't be even remotely like your life with him.'

No, she thought. Her life with William would be wonderful, a symphony of love and laughter, tenderness and joy, and running through it all the loyalty and strength of a real friendship.

The sobs rose again, but she buried them somehow.

'That's easy to say,' she told him, 'but it would be the same. In the end it would, anyway. That's just the way it is.'

'No. You're wrong. Give me a chance to prove it.'

'I can't,' she protested.

'You can. Please, Charlotte. You don't know what I've got at stake.'

'No,' she moaned.

'Please?' he asked, not pleadingly but quietly, from the heart. 'Give me some time—a couple of months, at least. We haven't known each other very long, I realise that. I know I'm sure, but I appreciate that it might take you longer to be certain, after what you've been through.'

That would take them to the end of January, and the end of her placement in Obs and Gynae. Until then they would be forced into each other's company anyway, an untenable situation if their relationship was ended.

This way perhaps she could slowly ease away, making the end less of a shock for them both.

'Maybe you're right,' she said unsteadily. 'Perhaps if we take it slowly, give it time—but I don't want you to get the wrong end of the stick. I'm not making any promises, William.'

He hugged her gently. 'OK. I'll try and be patient. I know what you've had to deal with, and I realise it can't be easy. Don't worry, I won't pressure you.'

He tipped her chin with a strong but gentle finger, and kissed her tenderly. 'I love you—just remember that.'

She wound her arms round his neck and hung on, unable to let go. She would have to lose him soon, she knew that, but she had him for now, and she would spend their time together building up a store of memories to take with her into her cold and lonely future.

*   *   *

The next few days were awful. Already considerate
and thoughtful, William became even more so, to the
point that Charlotte wished he would do something
wrong so that she could shout at him and ease the
tension.

One night after he had cooked a meal and she stood
up to clear the table he pushed her gently down again.
'You sit there; I'll do it.'

'But I want to do it,' she protested. 'For God's sake
stop waiting on me! I'm not paralysed!'

'I know that,' he said calmly. 'But you were on duty
last night; you must be tired.'

'And God forbid you should wear me out in the
kitchen so I'm no use in the bedroom,' she retorted.

His face drained of colour, and he sat down again,
staring at her.

'I don't believe you said that.'

Charlotte closed her eyes. She didn't believe she'd
said it, either, but if she was trying to put some distance
between them she couldn't have done it more effec-
tively.

'I'm sorry,' she mumbled.

'Do you really feel like that about our lovemaking?
That I'm using you?'

There was hurt in his voice—hurt and disbelief.
She couldn't let it go. Tears welled in her eyes
and she blinked them back. 'No, of course I don't.
I'm sorry; it's just conditioning. I know you're not
like that.'

He pulled her to her feet and into his arms.

'Come on, let's leave this lot and go and sit and talk.'

He led her into the sitting-room and tugged her down
beside him on the sofa, wrapping an arm round her
and easing her head against his chest.

'I don't want to talk,' she mumbled. 'Just hold me.'

'Oh, darling,' he said, his voice gentle. His hands cradled her against his chest, so that she could feel the steady thud of his heart, and she slipped her arms round his waist and snuggled closer. A weary sadness filled her, and, closing her eyes, she let it wash over her. He turned on some music with the remote control, and the pure, clear tones of a chorister flowed round them.

She didn't mean to cry, but the tears fell anyway, soaking into his shirt where it lay against her cheek.

'Charlotte?' he murmured.

'It's the music,' she said with a sniff, but he wasn't fooled.

Lifting her in his arms, he carried her up to the bedroom and made love to her, kissing away her tears. He was patient and gentle, his own desires savagely controlled, and when he finally let himself go the darkness rang with his words of love.

Charlotte thought that if a heart could truly break, then this was how it must feel, to be so near and yet so very, very far.

In addition to the strain of trying to convince her to marry him, William had the added burden of taking over the department and discovering all the untold horrors of Derek Blythe's reign.

To reduce his waiting lists, Derek had turned away patients who William felt should have been operated on. His first task as consultant was to write to the GPs of those patients he felt were a priority and recall them for further investigations. Inevitably this increased the workload, and to help with the resultant crisis Jo Carter came back as a locum, leaving Amy with Annie Hunter who was at home waiting for the arrival of her second child.

For Charlotte, working with Jo was both a blessing and a disappointment because, while it did give her a little emotional space and time away from William and their problems, the time it gave her was time she didn't really want.

Perverse though it was, she wanted to be with him every minute of the day. It hurt, of course, but then so did not being with him.

Fortunately they were busy, and as she worked alongside Jo, assuming more and more responsibility, she found she could distance herself from her personal problems provided she was kept sufficiently occupied—and that was hardly ever a problem.

By this time she had covered most of the commonly occurring obstetric problems, and Jo started teaching her some of the simple gynaecological procedures.

She started with a few routine D and Cs, learning how to dilate the cervix without damaging it, and how to use the curette to remove the lining of the uterus and any retained products of conception following spontaneous abortion.

She also performed her first hysterectomy under Jo's careful guidance.

The patient was a woman in her late forties with heavy bleeding from a mass of fibroids. It was a relatively simple operation, and Jo guided her through it letter by letter.

'Excellent—you're good. Well done,' Jo said as Charlotte closed, and she felt very satisfied.

'You're enjoying it, aren't you?' Jo commented afterwards as they left the theatre and went down for lunch.

'Yes, I am. It's fascinating.'

'Having second thoughts about general practice?'

Charlotte shook her head. 'No. I still want to be a GP. It's the variety. I think after a few years you must get a bit fed up with the same conditions.'

Jo laughed. 'Have you spoken to a GP recently? All they get are ingrowing toenails, tonsillitis and thrush.'

'And heart disease, and asthma, and antenatal, and paediatrics, and geriatrics, and——'

'OK, OK!' Jo threw up her hands and laughed again. 'You win. All we get are babies, heavy periods and cervical cancer.'

'And fibroids, and miscarriages, and terminations and ectopics and multiple pregnancies and ovarian cancer and teenage mothers!'

She looked at Jo, and saw the laughter drain from her eyes.

'And infertility. Don't forget that.'

Charlotte's smile faded. 'No. No, I won't forget that.'

'It's a very important part of the job, and it's a bit of a crusade of mine, for obvious reasons.'

'I'm sorry,' Charlotte said quietly.

Jo gave an expressive little shrug.

'That's OK. It's hardly your fault.'

'No,' Charlotte agreed. 'I realise that. It doesn't mean I don't care.'

Jo's smile was fleeting. 'Thanks.'

'It must hurt you, having it all going on around you all day and knowing it can never be.'

Jo shook her head. 'No—not any more. No more than seeing mothers with babies in the street and packets of condoms and sanitary towels in the super-market, and school playgrounds at dinnertime. Anyway, we've got Amy, and I couldn't ask for more. She's a lovely child, and we both adore her.'

Charlotte stirred her tea absently. 'How does Alex feel about it?'

'Alex? Oh, he's sad, as I am, but when he tells me now that he loves me I know he really means it. The worst thing was not feeling a real woman, but Alex has managed to convince me that I am, and he's right, of course. Our love is between us, not between us and our children.'

'But children are a part of it.'

'Yes,' Jo agreed, 'but not the main part. Children should be secondary to a relationship. I know that now, but it took me a while to really believe it was true. If a relationship is strong enough to withstand childlessness, it's strong enough to withstand the strain of being a parent! That's the interesting thing about people who adopt. They get divorced much less readily than parents raising their own natural children.'

'But if only one of you can't have them——'

'But that's always the case, or almost always. Sometimes there's a problem where the woman develops antibodies to her husband's sperm, but usually it's a mechanical or biological fault with one or the other. Even with the antibodies there's one person against the other, so to speak. So there's always an imbalance, a power shift. Ruthless people use it as a weapon, of course——Ah, here's William. Come and join us. Charlotte's been doing a textbook hysterectomy—she's got promise.'

'I know.' He grinned easily at them and slid into the seat beside Charlotte, winking at her.

'OK? Jo been looking after you? I'm sorry I've been so busy.'

Charlotte dredged up a smile. 'She's been wonderful; don't worry about it. How's it going?'

He groaned. 'Paperwork, following up the old man's mistakes and omissions—I'm going nuts. I shall have to have some more suits, as well. Power-dressing—I'm not sure I'm ready for it.'

Jo laughed. 'You'll enjoy it. Get Charlotte to go with you. Clothes shopping is always more fun with a friend.'

'Good idea. Saturday? Is Alex on take this weekend?'

'Yes,' Jo said. 'Worst luck. It's Amy's birthday and I wanted him at home.'

'Get Jake to do the weekend.'

'If Annie doesn't have the baby first.'

'Oh, God—we could be in anyway!' William said with a laugh. 'Oh, well, if I'm meant to look smart no doubt I'll get to the shops, and if not, well, they'll have to take me as they find me.'

Annie obligingly solved the problem of the weekend by going into labour on Thursday afternoon. She was right on time, her scan had shown the baby's head to be well down and with no disproportion, and no problems were anticipated.

However, she was terrified. Her first labour had been a disaster, the baby a 'stargazer', a face presentation that her pelvis was too tiny to deal with. Jake hadn't been there, hadn't even known the baby was his, and so she had had to cope alone through a terrifying ordeal that had come within an inch of tragedy.

This time she was determined it was going to be different. Jake was there, just as determined, and armed to the hilt with lavender and jasmine oils, jasmine and raspberry leaf teas, music and even a teddy of Beth's as a lucky mascot.

Her labour started slowly, and to relax her Bev Linari filled the water pool and encouraged her to get in it. 'You can always come out again and then go back in later,' she said, and so Annie spent a couple of hours in the warm water, floating peacefully while her labour did very little.

'She's come in really long before she needed to,' Bev told Charlotte and William who were in the ward office waiting for a progress report. 'Still, it's better to be on the safe side. When the cervix is open enough I'll give you a shout and you can decide if you think the presentation is straightforward or if she should have a section. She's tiny—I hadn't realised how dainty she is, really, till I examined her. How that idiot let her go on with a stargazer I just don't know.'

She headed for the door, then popped her head back round. 'You could always come in and play cards with her and help her pass the time—they're going to get awfully bored unless things pick up soon.'

William smiled. 'Typical Jake, panicking too early. Obstetricians always worry about their own wives far more than they do about other people's. I think sometimes when things go wrong Alex is almost glad Jo doesn't have to go through it.'

'I don't suppose he is, not really,' Charlotte said, thinking back to her conversation with Jo.

'No, I don't suppose he is, not deep down. I think he feels it very deeply for her.'

'What about himself?'

William shrugged. 'I don't think it's the same for men. There's the ego thing, of course, but Alex doesn't suffer from his ego. It's different for women. Childbirth is like some kind of rite of passage, a test you have to pass before you can join the sorority. It's a crippling burden to bear.'

Charlotte stood up abruptly. 'Shall we go and see how Annie's doing and cheerlead a bit?'

'Good idea.' William slid back his chair and straightened up, looking down at her. 'Are you OK?'

She nodded. 'Of course—I think the tension of this birth is getting to all of us. It's so important that it goes right for her.'

'It'll go right,' he said confidently. 'At least we don't have to hustle her so she's had it by the time the old man appears on the ward!'

A ghost of a smile touched Charlotte's face. 'Let's just hope his pessimism isn't justified.'

'What, you mean about my come-uppance? I hope so too. You do believe I don't take risks, don't you?'

She looked at him, at the serious expression on his face, the searching look in his eyes, and realised it was hugely important to him that she have faith in him.

'Yes, I do believe you don't take risks,' she said honestly. 'I think the problem with Blythe was that he realised your judgement was sounder than his.'

William laughed. 'You reckon? I don't agree—I think he genuinely thought I was reckless.'

'Well, I don't,' she said firmly.

Warmth touched his eyes. 'Thank you.'

She smiled. 'My pleasure. Now, let's go and see Annie.'

It was a long, slow night. They played cards, then when the contractions began to get closer together and more intense William examined her.

Charlotte wondered how Jake would feel, but he

had ceased to be an obstetrician and turned into a full-time father, complete with panic attacks.

'Well?' he asked. 'What sort of presentation is it?'

'Perfectly normal,' William said calmly. 'There shouldn't be any problem.'

'So why is it taking so long?'

William shrugged. 'How old is Beth?'

'Nearly nine,' Annie told him.

'So your body is completely back to normal. It will take time. That's fine. The baby's clearly not at all distressed, and there's absolutely no need to worry. You're about six centimetres dilated, so it will pick up soon. You're doing really well.'

'Oh, they are getting stronger—Jake?'

He reached for the jasmine oil, pouring some into his hands and rubbing it gently all over her back and down her hips and legs, working on the pressure-points on her feet and ankles as well.

'That's shiatsu,' Charlotte said in surprise.

'Uh-huh. It seems to work, so we thought we'd try it. Anything to make it better than last time.'

'It will be better than last time,' William said confidently.

'I hope so,' Annie muttered, coming out of the contraction. 'I think I'd like to go back in the water now.'

'Do you want us to go?' William asked, careful of her privacy.

'I don't care,' she said, and, stripping off her baggy T-shirt, she climbed carefully over the side of the pool, with Bev helping her and Jake hovering anxiously.

'Oh, that's fantastic. Oh, lovely. . .'

She rested her head back against the side, her hands smoothing rhythmically over her distended abdomen, and Jake worked on her shoulders and arms, then went round the other side and gave her feet some attention.

This time when she had her contraction she found the touch irritating, just wanting to be held, so Jake leant over the side and reached round her, holding her head against his shoulder and supporting her with his hands so that she could relax.

After another couple of contractions she began to panic.

'Jake?' she said.

'I'm here, darling.'

'I need you,' she sobbed. 'Where are you? I need you to hold me.'

'Why don't you get in the water with her?' Bev suggested.

Jake didn't hesitate. It was something fathers occasionally did, but Charlotte had never seen a man in the pool before. She wondered if he would feel silly, but it didn't occur to him; he was too busy trying to get close to Annie and support her.

It did seem to make a difference. He had wrenched off his shirt and trousers, kicked off his shoes and climbed in in his underwear, all within about fifteen seconds. He sat behind her, his arms round her so that she floated against him, and she relaxed visibly.

'Light breaths—that's it,' Bev encouraged, and Annie dropped her head back against Jake's broad shoulder and closed her eyes.

'Cold flannel,' she mumbled, and Bev handed Jake a flannel and he wiped her face tenderly.

'Better?'

'Thirsty.'

Bev passed a little sponge dipped in iced water, and Jake held it to her lips while she sucked it.

'Lovely,' she whispered, and he gave it back to Bev

and rested his hands lightly on her abdomen.

'Nearly there, darling,' he promised.

'Don't lie,' she mumbled. 'I want to go home.'

'Later. Let's do this first.'

'No. I don't want to.'

She tried to get out of the water but Jake stood up and held her, and she sank back down, beating against his chest.

'Ow—it hurts—let me go home!'

'Little breaths,' Bev said, but Annie was beyond hearing. She pummelled Jake's chest, grabbing handfuls of hair and yanking it, slapping her hands against his front and crying, all the time saying, 'Let me go home—let me go home.'

Jake met William's eyes over her head, his face stricken, and William smiled. 'She's in transition—she'll be in the second stage in a minute and this will all be over.'

'That's the bit I'm dreading,' he said quietly over Annie's sobbing head.

She had collapsed against him, her body shuddering, and seconds later she put her hand over her mouth and mumbled, 'Feel sick.'

Bev held a paper bowl under her chin and she retched, but then leant back against Jake. 'Oh, God, let me go home,' she pleaded.

'Darling, you're nearly there. You're in transition.'

'Oh, I'd forgotten how bloody it is. How did I let you talk me into this mess? Isn't Beth enough?' she sighed.

Jake's face was stricken, but Bev winked at him.

'She's fine,' she said. 'Everything's going really well. Don't listen to her; they all say things like that.'

'But she's right,' Jake said unsteadily. 'It was my

fault. I talked her into it, but never again. I'm having a vasectomy just as soon as I get out of this water.'

William chuckled. 'You're a case, Hunter,' he said genially. 'Bev, how's the baby's heart?'

Bev was listening to the baby's heartbeat with the waterproof ultrasound, and she nodded her satisfaction. 'A hundred and twenty-eight—that's lovely.'

'That means a boy,' Annie mumbled. 'They're always bigger.' She swore, briefly but comprehensively, and Jake blinked. Charlotte and William exchanged a look and both laughed under their breath.

Suddenly Annie seemed to gather her resources and straightened up. 'OK, folks, this is it,' she said, strangely calm, and, squatting in Jake's arms, propped against his chest, she took a steadying breath, pushed hard and let the breath out on a sigh. She breathed again, pushing harder but this time with an open epiglottis, so that a long, deep groan came from her throat. 'Come on, baby,' she muttered through gritted teeth, and then the tension left her and she leant back against Jake.

'OK?' he asked gently, smoothing her hair back from her brow with an unsteady hand.

'I'm fine. OK—this is it. Come on, baby—come on, come on—ah!'

Bev was reaching down into the water and Charlotte and William crowded round, desperate for the first glimpse of the new arrival.

'We've got a head—once more, Annie—lovely!'

Bev lifted the baby clear of the water and laid it on Annie's tummy, and Charlotte was amazed, as always, to see the smile that broke out on the new mother's face, the labour forgotten.

'Hello, darling,' Annie said reverently, and Jake

reached out a trembling hand and touched the baby for the first time.

Blue eyes stared up at him intently. 'Oh, God,' he said raggedly, and then nine months of tension and anticipation caught up with him. Dropping his face into Annie's shoulder, he sobbed as if his heart was breaking.

'I thought you were going to die,' he groaned, and Annie turned awkwardly and wrapped an arm around him.

'Silly twit,' she said affectionately. 'It was a breeze.'

'A breeze?' He lifted his head and stared at her. 'That's not what you were saying a minute ago.'

She shrugged. 'So I panicked. Look at your son.'

'It's a boy?' he asked, incredulous, and then the tears started again, mingled with laughter. 'Oh, hell, I'm sorry.'

William gave Jake a hand up, then he took the baby while Jake and Bev helped Annie out of the water on to a mattress beside the pool. Charlotte dried her shoulders with a towel and patted the ends of her hair which had trailed in the water, and Annie leant back against the pillows and sighed contentedly.

Then she noticed Jake.

'What happened to your chest?' she asked in horror.

It was scratched and reddened, and a thin trail of blood dribbled down through the hair.

He laughed wryly. 'You did.'

'I did that to you?' Her eyes were huge. 'When?'

'When you were trying to run away.'

She reached out a hand and touched him tenderly. 'Oh, darling, I'm sorry.'

He snorted. 'Here, do you want to hold this little fellow?'

While they waited for the placenta to come away, Annie offered the baby her breast, a tender smile on her lips. Jake knelt beside her, his face still streaked with tears, and shook his head in wonder.

He marvelled over the placenta, was stunned that Annie didn't need any stitches and couldn't take his eyes off his son for a second.

'What was his Apgar score?' he asked in a sudden emergence of the obstetrician he had briefly left behind.

'Eight at fifty-five seconds and ten at five minutes.'

Jake smiled, slowly at first, and then a radiant beam that seemed to light the room.

'Oh, I don't—I'm stunned.'

William laughed drily. 'We noticed.'

Annie looked up at them, her face tranquil. 'Thank you both for being here. I'm sorry we wasted your time.'

'I'm not,' William told them. 'It was just the way it should be. I just hope we didn't crowd you, but we couldn't bear to leave.'

Annie laughed. 'I didn't even notice you were here—I could have been in Piccadilly for all the notice I took of my surroundings. It's just such an incredibly focused process, somehow. So deeply—primitive? Your body takes over, as if nature has got control of it. It can be terrifying, but there's something so inherently right about it.'

'Shut up, Annie,' Jake told her. 'You were gibbering like an idiot and flaying me to shreds, and your language!'

She giggled like a naughty schoolgirl. 'Sorry, did I shock you?'

'Just a bit. I have a reputation, you know.'

'I don't think so,' William said with a smile. 'Not once I put these photos up on the notice board.'

Jake's face was a picture. 'Photos?'

'Of you in the water pool with Annie and the baby.'

'Let me see——'

'Uh-uh! I'll keep them, I think. You never know, I might want a favour.'

Jake laughed. 'Do your worst. It's the best moment of my life. I don't care what I look like.'

'Oh,' William said. 'Well, you'd better have them, then.'

He handed over a little stack of instant pictures, and Jake and Annie looked at them, laughing together.

'Oh, that's a lovely one,' Annie murmured.

It was one taken just as Jake touched his son for the first time, and all the love and wonder was there on his face for all to see.

'Come on, I think we've intruded enough,' William said softly, and putting his arm round Charlotte's shoulders, he led her out, leaving the little family alone.

CHAPTER NINE

'Do you think three's enough?'

Charlotte wriggled her toes inside her boots and sighed inwardly. He had tried on at least fifteen suits. The prospect of trying to find another defeated her. 'I'm sure it's enough,' she said with feeling.

'I wonder. Maybe I should have another sports coat or blazer and a couple of pairs of grey flannels or something—then I need shirts.'

'There's nothing wrong with the shirts you've got!' she exclaimed.

'Don't stop me, I'm on a roll,' he told her with an impish grin, and she sighed again, audibly this time.

'I thought women were bad,' she mumbled.

'Pardon?'

She dredged up an exasperated smile. 'Could we have a cup of coffee?'

He relented. 'Good idea—then we'll come back and tackle the rest.' He turned to the assistant. 'Could you keep this lot on one side? We're just going to refuel and we'll be back.'

Looping an arm around her shoulders, he steered her through the department store and up the escalators to the designer fashion floor where Charlotte had bought her dress the day William proposed.

I won't look at the wedding-dresses, she told herself sternly, and kept her eyes trained instead on William as they walked towards the restaurant.

'We ought to buy you a few more things while we're here,' he said, glancing round.

'I'll go to Marks and Spencer,' she said. 'Come on, there are some tables free.'

Just then there was a touch on her arm, and she stopped and turned.

'It is you, dear—are you feeling better? I was so worried.'

With shock Charlotte recognised the assistant from the bridal wear department.

'Yes, thank you, I'm fine now,' she said hastily, and started to step away.

'And is this the lucky man? He must be—congratulations.'

He frowned in puzzlement. 'Excuse me?'

'Your job—your fiancée said you'd been promoted. Perfect timing. Have you set the date yet? I've kept the dress.'

William looked confused, and Charlotte's eyes drooped shut. Get me out of here, she prayed.

'Oh, dear—have I put my foot in it?' the woman said worriedly. 'I'd better go.'

She patted Charlotte's hand anxiously, then fled.

'Charlotte? What was that about?'

'Nothing. Come on, let's have coffee.'

'Not until you tell me what she was on about.'

'I tried on a dress,' she said, flannelling furiously. 'She said she'd keep it for me.'

'What was that about setting the date? And why did she think we were engaged?'

Charlotte shrugged. 'She must have got the wrong end of the stick.'

'So why is my promotion perfect timing? Perfect timing for what?'

He wasn't going to give up. Charlotte swallowed, biting her lips to regain her composure. 'She misunderstood. I didn't want to disappoint her.'

'So?'

'So I tried on a dress.'

William looked over her head, following the woman as she crossed the floor to the bridal wear.

'A wedding-dress?'

His voice was softer, touched with hope, and suddenly it was all too much.

'Yes, a wedding-dress,' she said, fighting tears. 'A wedding-dress for a wedding I can't have.'

He was silent for a moment, then his arm went round her shoulders and he turned her towards the lift.

'Where are we going?' she asked numbly.

'Home, so we can talk about this properly.'

'What about your suits?'

'To hell with my suits.'

He was silent the rest of the way home, and once they were in and the door was closed he headed for the kitchen.

'Coffee?' he asked.

She lifted her shoulders helplessly. 'I don't care.'

He came back to her, drawing her gently into his arms, then led her into the sitting-room and pushed her down on to the settee, coming down beside her.

'Now, let's talk. What did you mean, a wedding-dress for a wedding you can't have?'

'You know I can't marry you,' she said, her voice choked and rusty.

'I don't know any such thing. When did you try the dress on?'

'Two weeks ago, when you asked me to marry you.'

'What, you just went in there afterwards and tried it on?'

She shook her head. 'No, before. I was in there getting the blue dress for that evening, and the wedding-dresses just caught my eye.'

'And?'

'Well, and nothing. I was just being silly. I don't know what I was thinking about. You hadn't even asked me at that point. Anyway, there was this one dress, and before I knew where I was I was trying it on and telling her all about you and pretending——' She broke off, quelling the sobs, and looked down at her fingers twisting together on her lap. 'You said yourself anyone can dream. That's all I was doing— just allowing myself to pretend, just for a while. I didn't think it would hurt anybody. . .'

'But you don't have to dream,' he said gently. 'You can marry me as soon as you want. Charlotte, I don't understand. If you want to get married, we can—we can do it next week.'

'But I can't—William, I mustn't! Oh, God, you don't understand!'

'Charlotte, I'm not Greg.'

'This isn't anything to do with Greg! He's just a red herring.'

'Marriage, then. Is that what you're afraid of? That once I'd got you I'd revert to type?'

She shook her head. 'No—oh, no, William—I know you wouldn't. You're the first man in my life who didn't think it was my inalienable right to serve him. I know damn well you'd be a wonderful husband.'

William sighed. 'So what's the problem, Charlotte? Damn it, woman, tell me! I think after all we've been through I deserve the truth!'

She lifted her head and looked at him through ravaged eyes. 'Yes, you do,' she said unsteadily. 'The thing is—it's just—I can't give you children. I'm sterile—barren.'

Shock drained the colour from his face, and then his arms were round her, cradling her against his chest.

'I'll kill him,' he said savagely, his voice trembling with emotion. 'I'll find him and I'll kill him. Where the hell did you get a word like barren?'

'The same place I got the word frigid,' she told him expressionlessly.

'Oh, Charlotte,' he said, his voice rich with compassion.

It was her undoing. Wrapping her hands in the folds of his shirt, she buried her face in his chest and cried as if her heart was broken.

He let her cry, holding her gently, smoothing her hair and murmuring wordless comfort until she grew calm.

Then he tipped back her chin, wiped her eyes and kissed her.

'I still love you,' he told her quietly. 'I still want to marry you. It doesn't make any difference.'

'Of course it does! Look at this place! You even told me why you bought it!'

'It's just a house,' he said.

'No, it isn't! It's a *family* house! It's got five bedrooms—damn it, we could sleep in a different one almost every night!'

'You're being silly about the house——'

'No, I am not! I'm being honest. You bought it because you want children. I can't give you children.'

'We could adopt or foster if you wanted to.'

She turned and looked at him, searching for the pain

and disillusion. She couldn't find it. 'It's not me,' she said, watching him for his reaction, 'it's you. You're the one who'll lose out, admit it.'

He sighed. 'OK. I admit, I'd like children. I've always thought in terms of having them one day, mainly, I think, because I felt I'd be able to love them. I never thought I'd ever love another woman, not with the sort of blind devotion I felt for Eleanor.' He smiled wryly at Charlotte. 'You rather caught me by surprise.'

'Do you love me like that?' she asked wistfully. 'With blind devotion?'

He shook his head. 'No. I'm older now, and wiser maybe. I can see your faults, and my own, and I still love you. Devotion, yes, but not blind. There's no question of me one day waking up and seeing you as you really are and wondering what the hell I'm doing with you. Our marriage will be far, far stronger than that.'

'But I can't marry you!' she protested.

'What tests have you had?' he asked, changing tack.

'Tests?'

'Tests—to find out what's wrong.'

She stared at him. 'None—why should I?'

'So how do you know it's you? Why not Greg?'

'I saw the result of his sperm count—don't worry, he made sure I knew it was me.'

'Did they do a post-coital test?'

She shook her head, embarrassed to be discussing her previous relationship like this, but he was undeterred.

'You haven't had a laparoscopy—no, I would have seen the scars.'

'I haven't had any tests,' she repeated. 'There was no point.'

'So you have no idea what's wrong?'

She shook her head again. 'No.'

'Well, I think it's time to have some. There might be damn all wrong with you. Why didn't you want to find out?'

'Why?' she asked simply. 'I didn't think I'd ever need to know—marriage to him was so awful I couldn't see myself ever being in a situation where I loved someone enough to want to have his children.'

'And now?'

His face was grave, mirroring his uncertainty of her. She reached up, cupping his cheek in her hand. 'You must know how much I love you—how much I ache every time a woman gives birth and I see the joy on her partner's face, and I know I'll never see that joy on your face——'

His eyes filled with tears, and he wrapped her in his arms and cradled her tenderly against his heart.

'Oh, Charlotte—I thought you didn't love me.'

'Not love you? How could I not love you? You mean everything to me. Oh, God, William, I want your baby so much it hurts me inside. . .'

'Oh, my darling——'

His voice broke, and she felt his chest heave under her cheek. He's crying for me, she thought in wonder. How can he care so much for me?

They clung to each other, sharing the sorrow, and then he lifted his head and looked down at her. 'Go and get the dress,' he said softly. 'We'll get married as soon as we can, and we'll sort out some tests for you.'

'No. I'll have the tests first—in case.'

'In case what? They aren't going to find anything that'll make me change my mind. I love you, and I want to marry you and spend my life with you. Whether or not we're blessed with children is another question entirely.'

'No, it isn't.'

'Yes, it is. Now go and wash your face and I'll get us some coffee, and we'll go back and put that poor woman out of her misery.'

She sniffed. 'And the man with the suits.'

'Him, too. Go on, there's a good girl.'

So they went back to the store, and William hovered around the displays while Charlotte bought the dress and the veil and the headband, and tried on shoes and a strapless bra and did her best to reassure the agitated woman.

'I was so worried—he looked confused, and you looked so stricken, I wondered what on earth I'd done.'

Charlotte smiled. 'You brought us together—he'd asked me to marry him and I'd said no. You see, I can't have children. Anyway, he knows that now, and he wants to marry me anyway.'

'Quite right too,' the assistant said firmly. 'My husband and I have never had any children, but we've had a wonderful marriage for nearly forty years. Oh, thank goodness I said something—just imagine, you might have thrown it all away!'

Charlotte hugged her impulsively. 'Yes, I might. I'm so grateful I can't tell you.' She looked at the gown and all the accessories, and bit her lip worriedly. 'You don't think this is going a bit far for a second wedding, do you? He's widowed and I'm divorced—maybe I should just settle for a little suit.'

'No. Absolutely not. You look so lovely in the dress, and I can tell by your face that he's the man for you. You mustn't count the first one. This is your real wedding.'

Charlotte smiled. She couldn't help herself. There was a little bubble of happiness inside her that just refused to be kept down. 'You're right,' she agreed. 'This is my real wedding.'

She signed the cheque without allowing herself to think about the expense, and, gathering up the boxes and bags, she thanked the woman again.

'My pleasure, dear,' she said, and as Charlotte turned away she could have sworn she saw a tear gleam in her eye.

'All done?' William asked her.

'I hope so. I seem to have bought everything in there.'

He chuckled and took the parcels from her. 'Let's go and put them in the car and come back for my suits, or we won't be able to carry them.'

So they did, and they had lunch in the restaurant, and by the time William had acquired another suit, two pairs of trousers and a sports jacket Charlotte had a raging headache.

'Let's go home,' she said, and for the first time it sounded right.

News of their engagement travelled through the hospital like wildfire. They saw the hospital chaplain who agreed to marry them in the little chapel, and they went and saw the registrar and got a special licence.

Julia Carmichael was on the following weekend, and so they agreed to reschedule the Friday clinic and fixed the wedding for four o'clock on the Friday afternoon. That way they would have the weekend at least to themselves.

That took care of Monday. William had already phoned his parents, and they were absolutely delighted, demanded to speak to Charlotte and were so kind and welcoming that it brought tears to her eyes—yet again.

'I'm turning into a watering can,' she told William as she put the phone down.

In fact she felt weepy the whole time—weepy and tired and generally out of sorts. On Tuesday morning she felt sick with fright just thinking about the wedding and the commitment William was making to her, despite the unknown reason for her infertility.

She was working with Jo again, and broached the subject cautiously.

'Would you do me a favour?' she said over coffee, midway through a clinic.

Jo looked puzzled. 'Sure—what? Something to do with the wedding?'

'Indirectly. Could you find out why I can't have children?'

Jo's face registered first shock, then understanding. 'I thought you were pretty hot on the empathy,' she said gently. 'Oh, Charlotte. Tell me about it.'

Charlotte shrugged. 'There's not a lot to tell. My ex-husband had a slightly low sperm count, but quite within the normal range. That's all I know.'

'What does William say?'

'Get married and then have the tests. I wanted to do it the other way round.'

Jo shook her head. 'No. If he only wanted you for the children, you wouldn't have a marriage, and it wouldn't be William. He's not like that.'

Charlotte's face softened in a smile. 'I know. Sometimes I wonder what he sees in me.'

Jo laughed. 'Maybe a registrar he can rely on?'

Charlotte chuckled, then sobered. 'It's an idea.

Do you think it smacks of nepotism?'

'Inevitably, but I shouldn't worry. There are lots of husband and wife teams in the hospital. Ask him, if you don't want to do general practice any more.'

'I'm not sure. I've found obs and gynae so rewarding, despite the ache.'

They exchanged an understanding smile, and then went back to the clinic where Charlotte toyed with the idea of changing her specialism.

Would she be able to cope with it?

With William's support, maybe. She found she wanted to try.

That afternoon Charlotte found herself delivering a pre-term baby. William was in Theatre and Jo, who was only filling in part-time, had gone home to Amy. She was working alongside Sue Coulter, and they were trying to give the baby the gentlest possible birth.

It was ten weeks early, only three-quarters of the way through its preparation for the world, and Andrew Barrett was with them waiting.

Progress was slow, however, and while Andrew went back to his clinic for a while they nipped out for a cup of tea on the ward, leaving the mother with her husband and a student midwife.

'Will you rupture the membranes?' Charlotte asked Sue.

'Oh, no. We never rupture the membranes of prem babies,' Sue told her. 'If they can be born "in caul", the forewaters act as a wedge to dilate the cervix and prepare the birth canal, and it takes the strain off the baby's delicate skull.'

'I thought it used to be standard practice to use forceps to guard the head.'

'It was,' Sue told her. 'Till Alex and William. They leave the membranes with breech babies as well, because their bodies are so small they can get entrapment of the head as it follows. The intact membranes reduce the chance of that and also protect against cord prolapse.'

'So why were they ever ruptured?' Charlotte asked in amazement.

Sue laughed. 'Do you want a historical or a political answer?'

'Neither. How about this baby? Can you tell yet if it's a breech or vertex presentation?'

'Oh, it's vertex,' Sue said confidently. 'There shouldn't be a problem, except for the gestational age. William's around if necessary, I take it.'

Charlotte shook her head. 'He's in Theatre. If you think we'll need him we ought to call him early rather than late.'

'We'll manage. I think it will be quite straightforward.'

It was, in fact, and very gentle. It was a second baby, and the mother pushed only with great care, pausing when Sue told her and allowing the baby's tiny head to be born without any expulsive effort.

Andrew was there immediately Sue ruptured the membranes, sucking the baby out and intubating it without waiting for the placenta to be delivered.

The cry was weak and tore through Charlotte, but Andrew was pleased with it and allowed the mother to hold her tiny daughter for a moment before hurrying her off to SCBU in an incubator.

'You can go and see her as soon as we've got you sorted out,' Sue promised, and sent the husband off with Andrew to be with the baby while she dealt with the placenta and the student midwife gave the mother a wash and changed her into her nightie. Then she was wheeled up to the little area by SCBU reserved for mothers of prem babies, and was allowed to see her baby again.

'It must be agony worrying about them for the next few days and weeks until they know,' Charlotte said to Sue.

'Awful. I don't think I could stand it. Some of them stay there day after day, just waiting for their babies to die. It's so sad it turns me over.'

'Maybe that baby will be all right,' Charlotte said hopefully.

'Oh, I'm sure it will. That lovely careful delivery we were able to achieve will make a huge difference to any neurological problems.'

There was nothing to be done for a baby born the following day, however. It was anencephalic, a fact which had been undetected because the mother had refused a scan and because the usual symptom, hydramnios or a large amount of fluid around the baby, had been absent.

Sue Coulter called Charlotte when the membranes ruptured, because the amount of fluid triggered her instincts.

'I think we need William for this, and also a paediatrician. I think there's something nasty wrong.'

William came immediately from Gynae where he was talking to a post-operative patient. 'Any history, anything to indicate what it might be?' he asked Sue.

'Nothing. It's her second baby, full term—nothing abnormal that I can find, nothing in the notes. She did seem a bit big, but she's a little obese so it's hard to be accurate about it.'

William nodded. 'OK. What have you told her?'

'Nothing yet.'

'OK. Well, let's run through the options. It could be spina bifida, oesophageal atresia, anencephaly, diabetes in the mother, twins—any one of a number of things. We won't know until the baby's born, so we need to warn them gently that something may be not quite right, without terrifying them. And it could be nothing. Polyhydramnios can be very difficult to diagnose. Let's just see her and have a chat as if nothing's wrong, and then we'll watch it very carefully from there. I don't suppose we've got time to scan her?'

Sue shook her head. 'No, she's too far down.'

The labour proceeded quite quickly, but as the cervix dilated Sue detected an abnormality of the baby's skull.

'Sue thinks it's anencephaly,' Charlotte told William on the phone.

'Oh, hell,' he said softly. 'Can you deal with it, or would you like me to come down?'

She swallowed. 'I think I'd like you to come down, if you can spare the time.'

'Of course. Hang on, I'll be with you in a moment. Don't go back in there.'

He appeared less than a minute later, and, giving her a reassuring smile and a hug, he led her into the delivery-room.

'We're a little concerned because you've had quite a lot of fluid round the baby,' he told the parents gently. 'That could indicate a problem, but what sort of problem we aren't sure yet. However, it seems likely that there could be something wrong with the baby. I'd like to examine you and see how you're getting on, and then I'd like to call a paediatrician down to be here for the birth, so we can have an expert opinion.'

The couple exchanged stunned glances. 'What sort of thing wrong?' the mother asked anxiously. 'You don't mean anything drastic, do you?'

'We aren't sure,' William said. 'Let me examine you first, then I'll see if I can give you a clearer idea.'

He washed his hands and pulled on some gloves, then gently, almost reverently, he examined her, his face expressionless.

When he withdrew his hand and tugged off the gloves, he sighed softly. 'I'm sorry,' he told them. 'I can't be sure at the moment. We'll have to wait until it's born—it won't be long now.'

The mother sobbed quietly. 'Oh, God, no,' she moaned. 'Please, no.'

Charlotte caught William's eye, and he shook his head very slightly.

Her heart sank. They were going to have a tragedy.

She went out and called Andrew Barrett, and he came and stood quietly in the delivery-room, a big and gentle man, his presence strangely reassuring.

When the baby was born a few minutes later, Charlotte could see that although the face was quite normal the baby's head was much smaller than it should have been, because the vault of the skull was missing.

Its cry was weak and mewling, and Andrew's face told them the news.

'I'm afraid that your baby has a condition called anencephaly,' he told them gently. 'That means that the skull hasn't formed properly, and unfortunately neither has the brain. It's a neural tube defect, like spina bifida, but it's tragically always fatal.'

'Fatal?' the mother echoed, aghast. 'You mean the baby will die?'

'I'm afraid so.'

She turned to her husband, her face ravaged with shock. 'Phil?'

'Isn't there anything that can be done?'

Andrew shook his head. 'Hold her—she's beautiful. She needs you.'

The mother looked at the baby, her eyes welling with tears, and, reaching out her arms, she cradled the dying baby against her breast.

'Can I feed her?'

He shook his head. 'She won't suckle. The reflex is missing.'

Sue went about her job of delivering the placenta after the unusual step of administering syntocinon to make the uterus contract. Post-partum haemorrhage was a complication of polyhydramnios, because of the over-distention of the uterus, but with the use of the drug strong contractions could be encouraged.

Charlotte tried to remember other facts, other figures, anything other than focus on what was happening in the room in front of her eyes.

As they stood there, the chaplain came into the room and baptised the baby at the parents' request. Then, as if it was now all right to do so, the little scrap lost her tenuous hold on life and slipped quietly away.

Later William comforted Charlotte as they sat in his sitting-room.

'You have to learn to take the rough with the smooth,' he said gently. 'But that was pretty grim.'

'It was actually very peaceful,' Charlotte said, still surprised at how natural the baby's death had seemed.

'Yes. It was natural. I'm glad you can see that.'

'We expect everything to be perfect all the time,' she said. 'That's why reality is so hard.'

She wondered, for the hundredth time, how they would cope once the reality of her infertility was proved once and for all.

Perhaps they wouldn't. Perhaps she would lose William yet.

The thought made her feel sick with terror.

CHAPTER TEN

WILLIAM'S parents arrived on Thursday evening for the wedding, and took them both out for a meal to the floating Italian restaurant where they had gone the night William proposed.

This time, however, they enjoyed themselves.

Charlotte wore the silk jersey dress that William had all but ripped off her the last time she had worn it, and although he behaved himself in the presence of his parents his eyes were more than expressive enough.

His father, too, made appreciative noises, and Judith told them both off for embarrassing her.

'Poor girl,' she admonished them, and then gave her a hug. 'You look gorgeous. I'm dying to see the dress tomorrow.'

Charlotte felt her butterflies leap into action again. 'I just hope I don't look ridiculous in a real wedding-dress at my age.'

'Your age?' Michael exclaimed. 'What are you, twenty-six?'

'Twenty-seven.'

'Scandalous.'

William's lips twitched, and Judith glared at him.

'Anyway, how could you possibly look ridiculous?' she said pragmatically. 'It *is* a real wedding. Who's going to help you get ready for it?'

Charlotte stared at her blankly. 'I hadn't thought about it.'

'I'm afraid I haven't given her a great deal of

time to prepare for it,' William said wryly.

'Afraid she'd change her mind?' Michael said with a chuckle, but William nodded, his face serious.

'I was. I still am. I'll believe it when she's married me.'

Charlotte stared at him in amazement. 'You know I wouldn't back out now.'

'Do I?' he asked.

She reached for him blindly across the table.

'Of course—William, I love you!'

'I love you too—God, if you only knew how much.'

There was a discreet cough from his father. 'Would you like us to leave, or shall we just change places so you can get at each other?'

William started to laugh. 'Sorry, I forgot you were here.'

'Hmm. Good job I reminded you before you really embarrassed yourselves.'

Charlotte blushed, William laughed and Judith smiled contentedly.

'So, Charlotte, answer the question. Who is going to help you get ready?'

'Um—my sister's coming up in the morning. She lives in London. I suppose she will.'

William grinned. 'The sister who gave you the perfume?'

She bit her lips to hide the smile. 'I've only got one—Linda.'

'Good,' he said in satisfaction. 'I get to thank her at last. I wonder what she'll give you for a wedding-present?' he added with a wicked twinkle.

'Probably a set of handcuffs to chain you to the sink with—she's into women's lib. In fact, you'll probably get on very well. I don't think I've been allowed to wash so much as a teaspoon yet.'

Judith chuckled. 'He was well-trained, dear. It wasn't an accident, believe me!'

They went over the final plans for the wedding, then William took her home, kissing her lingeringly.

'I want to make love to you,' he told her with a groan.

'Tough. I need my beauty sleep, and so do you. We've both got to work in the morning.'

'Mmm. Do something for me?'

'What?' She slid her hands up his chest, feeling for his heart. It raced against her palm.

'Wear Linda's perfume—lots of it. We may only have the weekend, but I intend to make the best possible use of every second.'

She grinned impishly. 'Oh, yes?'

'Oh, yes. Don't bother to pack much; I don't intend to leave the hotel room at all.'

She stared at him. 'Hotel room? What hotel room?'

He tapped the side of her nose. 'Never you mind— secret. Now, if you're refusing to pander to me, I suppose I'd better go.'

He dropped a light kiss on her lips, then let himself out, leaving her alone with her nerves.

She slept badly, and in the morning the rich food of the night before and the worry about her tests and what they would reveal took their toll. She lost her breakfast before she left for work, and it was only once she was caught up in the frenzy that she forgot herself enough to feel better.

Bev collared her when she entered the ward.

'We've got a nasty delivery—a big baby, and it's a stargazer. I've alerted William, and he wants to let the mother try for a while, but he's had to go and start the clinic. He wanted you to stay here to be on the safe side.'

Charlotte pulled on her white coat and followed Bev towards the delivery suite.

'How does he want to play it? Will he do an episiotomy?'

'I shouldn't think so. The baby's face is going to pull the cervix right down to the perineum, which will protect the wall of the vagina to some extent. It may stop her getting bladder problems later on in life. The back wall is more likely to tear with the chin coming through, and he wants her to deliver squatting on all fours to take the strain off the perineum a bit. Frankly, the fuss she's making already, I think we'll have a job making her push lying flat on her back!'

They went into the labour-room and found the patient, a woman in her early twenties, moaning and clutching her husband. 'It hurts—it hurts!' she was saying, and Charlotte's heart reached out to her.

'What about pain relief?'

'She's had pethidine—I want to get her in the water but hospital policy excludes malpresentation.'

'Maybe for a while?' Charlotte said. 'Should I go down and ask William?'

'It's bad luck to see the groom on your wedding-day,' Bev said. 'Ring him.'

Charlotte didn't care in the least about superstition. She just didn't want to lose a baby on her wedding-day. She phoned the clinic, though, because it was quicker, and William suggested putting the mother in the water as long as the baby wasn't distressed.

'Get Bev to check the heartbeat every three minutes,' he said, 'and at the peak of every contraction.

I'll be up in about an hour—Jo's coming in; she's going to take over.'

So she would see him anyway. She felt instantly happier.

The woman was nervous about going in the water, but once in there relaxed immediately.

'Oh, it feels wonderful,' she said with a sigh, and with her next contraction, although it was clearly still very painful, she made much less fuss.

'That's better,' Bev said. 'The baby likes it too— the heartbeat didn't dip so much. The pressure's off, I guess.'

The labour progressed slowly, and was obviously very hard work. She went into the second, expulsive stage, and William arrived and decided to leave her in the water but with almost constant attention.

Bev used the Sonicaid to monitor the baby's heartbeat constantly, and although it dipped during contractions it picked up again well afterwards.

'It's a good, strong baby,' he said encouragingly.

'It's huge,' the mother moaned. 'I'll never get it out. I'm going to die – aaaah!'

William, his sleeves rolled right up, reached down into the water and quickly examined her.

'It's very close, but not progressing. I think we need to get you out, get a bit of gravity working and may be use the ventouse extractor to help you a bit.'

They lifted her out, protesting and moaning, and then Bev positioned her so that she was squatting with her feet on the floor and her hands on the side of the pool.

The baby's face was visible, almost crowning, and William rigged up the ventouse and then knelt down behind her.

'This isn't going to be the easiest thing to get on, but I don't want to lay her down now. Ok, Jackie, I'm going to put the suction cup on the baby's head now and then we can help you when you push, all right?'

There was a moan from the mother, and William, working by touch alone, managed to position the cup at the second attempt.

With the next contraction the baby's heartbeat dropped alarmingly, and didn't pick up.

'Right,' William said. 'Jackie, push, love, as hard as you can—now.'

The mother pushed, William pulled and wriggled, and suddenly the head popped free, followed immediately by the rest of the baby and all the amniotic fluid.

They were all soaked, but the baby took their attention off the fact.

He was huge, very much alive and extremely indignant.

Jackie sat down with a plonk, and so did her husband.

'Well,' they said, and stared at him.

William straightened up, looked at Charlotte and smiled.

'I'll finish off here—I suggest you go and get ready. Much as I love obstetrics, I draw the line at marrying you with amniotic fluid in your hair.'

The wedding was lovely. Everyone from the obstetrics team was there, bar none. Linda had arrived and helped Charlotte to get ready, exclaiming over her dress and saying all the right things.

'You've actually got a bit of a chest!' she teased.

Charlotte laughed. 'It's the dress—it works miracles. Here, help me with the veil.'

They fixed it, and then Charlotte stood back and twirled in front of the mirror.

'Will I do?'

'Do?' Linda smiled mistily. 'Sis, you look terrific.'

'Thanks.' Charlotte bit her lip, nerves attacking her again. 'Oh, God, I feel sick with fright.'

'You always were a worrywart. You'll be fine.'

The car arrived and took them to the hospital, and they found William's parents waiting.

'Here—I made you a bouquet,' Judith said, and handed her a lovely spray of lilies and freesias. The smell was intoxicating, and Charlotte smiled. William would like it. She thanked Judith.

Then Michael stepped forward. 'I don't suppose you've thought of this either, but who's giving you away?'

Charlotte's face clouded. 'I don't know.'

'Well, I don't wish to presume, but if I might offer my services?'

Charlotte took the proferred arm and hung on tight. 'Thank you.'

'My pleasure. Are you ready?'

She nodded.'

'You look beautiful, by the way. My son's a very lucky man.'

The others preceded them into the little chapel, and when the organist began the introduction of 'Here comes the Bride' Charlotte took a steadying breath and stepped forward into her new life.

'Are you OK? You haven't eaten very much.'

'I'm just nervous,' she told William. 'I picked at the reception.'

'You look tired—how about an early night?'

They were in the honeymoon suite of an exclusive hotel, once a magnificent country house, and Charlotte looked across the room at the huge bed draped in acres of white silk. It looked immensely appealing. She felt absolutely exhausted.

'Good idea,' she said, and so William helped her to undress and then sent her into the bathroom ahead of him.

By the time he had finished in there after her, she was curled up in the bed asleep. With a wry smile he slipped in beside her, eased her into his arms and joined her in oblivion.

They woke early, to the sound of birds outside the window.

'Good morning,' he murmured.

'Mmm.' She snuggled into his side and kept her eyes shut. She felt thoroughly hung-over and sick.

'Tea?' he said, and, throwing back the bedclothes, she ran for the bathroom.

Seconds later he was there beside her, perched on the edge of the bath holding her head while she retched.

She sagged against him, and he tore off a piece of toilet tissue and blotted her mouth. She sank on to the side of the bath and leant against him, feeling totally wiped out.

'Are you OK now?' he asked gently.

She nodded. 'Mmm. I thought it would have stopped now the wedding's over. I was so scared—I thought it was the wedding, but it must be worrying about the tests.'

'Hmm.' William scooped her up into his arms and carried her back into the bedroom, placing her carefully on the bed. Then he rang Room Service and asked for an apple, some crackers and some iced mineral water.

He washed her face, then there was a knock at the door and he opened it, taking the tray from the bellboy and setting it on the bedside table.

Charlotte watched him, bemused.

'What's that for?' she asked listlessly.

'You. Here.'

He gave her a cracker, then a sip of mineral water to wash it down. 'Better?'

'Mmm. Can I have another?'

He passed her one, watching her eat it with a strange expression on his face, then handed her the drink again.

'Can I ask you something?' he said.

She blinked. 'Of course.'

'When was your last period?'

'My last——? Heavens.' She tried to think. 'I don't know—just after your interview.'

'Five and a half weeks ago.'

'Is it?'

He nodded. 'Have you noticed anything other than nausea?'

'Like?'

'Tiredness?'

She nodded.

'Tender breasts, maybe a little bigger?'

She nodded again, her mind groping for an answer. 'What's wrong with me?' she asked, suddenly afraid.

He smiled, a tentative, tender smile. 'Nothing. I think you're pregnant.'

'Preg——But I can't be pregnant!'

'Why not?'

'Because I——' She broke off. She had no reason,

nothing she could put her finger on and say, This is why.

'There could have been dozens of reasons why you didn't have Greg's baby. I don't care what they were. I think—I'm sure—you're going to have mine.'

Charlotte's hand slid down over her tummy and settled in the bowl of her pelvis. It felt flatter than ever, and it seemed impossible that there could be a baby there.

'You're wrong—you must be,' she said scratchily. 'I can't——'

'I'll get a test,' he said. 'Stay here; I'll be back in a while.'

He dressed quickly, then went out. Half an hour later he was back, a home pregnancy test in his pocket.

'It may not work so soon—you're only ten days late,' he told her.

'It won't work,' she said heavily, but she got out of bed and took the thing into the bathroom, closing the door firmly in his face.

A few minutes later she emerged, her face incredulous.

'It says—I must be——Oh, William, we're going to have a baby!'

And, throwing herself into his arms, she burst into tears.

'Come on, perk up, or they'll think I'm making you do all sorts of awful things against your will,' he teased, and she giggled tearfully and hugged him again.

Happiness flooded through her. At least it felt like happiness, and it was certainly flooding. It kept leaking out of her eyes, despite all her efforts at stopping it, and in the end William just picked her up and carried her to the bed.

'Do you feel up to celebrating?' he asked softly.

Her arms wound round his neck, drawing him down. 'Oh, yes—definitely.'

'Good, because I don't think I can bear to watch you cry any more and it might take your mind off it.'

She giggled, as she was meant to, and tugged off his jumper over his head.

He dispatched the jeans and came back beside her with a sigh. 'Oh, Charlotte. What a wedding-present.'

'I don't believe it. I keep pinching myself.'

'No wonder you're crying.'

She laughed again, and, reaching for him, drew him into her arms. 'I love you, William.'

'I love you too—so very, very much.'

His lips covered hers, exquisitely gentle, and her tears were forgotten. . .

EPILOGUE

CHARLOTTE lay propped up on the pillows at William's side, watching as his hand trailed idly over the smooth swell of her abdomen.

'I wonder what it is?' she said quietly.

'Do you mind?'

She shook her head. 'No—not for me. For you, maybe.'

He laid his hand over the baby. 'Why for me?'

She shrugged expressively. 'I thought you'd want a boy.'

He studied her, his eyes gentle, then shook his head. 'I don't mind. Having a boy won't give me my son back, Charlotte. I know that. Whatever we have, my only concern is that you should both be all right, and everything looks fine.'

'We'll know next week.'

'Mmm.' He bent forward and pressed his lips to her skin. 'Hello, baby,' he murmured, and he was rewarded with a little kick. A smile touched the corner of his mouth. 'Nothing wrong with you, is there?'

He lifted his head and met Charlotte's eyes, his own intent. 'How are you feeling?'

She smiled knowingly. 'Fine. Why?'

He shrugged nonchalantly. 'I wondered if you felt like any more prostaglandin therapy.'

He couldn't quite keep the impish quirk from his lips, and she stroked a finger down his nose and patted his smile. He had informed her a few days ago that semen contained a high concentration of natural prostaglandin, the substance used to induce labour. He had repeated the treatment as frequently as he could cope with ever since, to Charlotte's delight and amusement.

She decided to indulge him—and herself—again. 'I should think so,' she told him casually, 'but at this rate my cervix will be so ripe, the baby will fall out.'

'Are you complaining?'

'About the treatment? Never.' She smiled and reached for him. 'Absolutely not. Come here.'

He was gentle—she was too near the end for anything but the most careful lovemaking—but his touch still drove her wild, and left her slaked and boneless at his side.

Finally, reluctantly, he levered himself away from her, dropping a light kiss on her brow. 'I have to go—my new SHO starts today.'

'Don't give him a hard time.'

She watched him as he left the bed, his body strong and lean, lightly tanned from lazing in the garden. He went to shower and came back, dressing quickly before kissing her goodbye and running down the stairs. The front door slammed behind him.

Closing her eyes, she snuggled back down the bed and sighed with contentment.

She woke an hour later to a dull ache, low down across her abdomen. It spread, then faded, then a little later came back, stronger this time but still gentle, still easily manageable.

She got up and washed, dressed herself and called a taxi. The contractions were too close together to wait for William, and anyway he had the new SHO to deal with. Bev could look after her for a while. She phoned her.

Her case was ready in the hall, and the taxi driver picked it up and helped her into the car.

Bev met her at Reception and walked with her to the lift.

'William will be so cross with you,' she scolded gently.

Charlotte smiled. 'I'm fine. I'll ring him when I'm up there.'

Bev snorted. 'We'll see. Do you have a birth plan?'

Charlotte laughed. 'Do you really think once William knows I'll be allowed any say?'

'Don't you worry, I'll sort him out,' Bev promised. 'Now, any plans?'

'I'd like a water birth.'

Bev smiled. 'I thought so. I've run the pool.'

As they were walking down the corridor she caught sight of William with a young, nervous-looking doctor.

'The new SHO. He'll do—he looks scared of us.'

Charlotte laughed, and William's head came up.

'What the——?'

'A new patient—would you like me to clerk her, sir?' the SHO asked.

'Clerk——? No—I'll do it; she's my wife,' William said over his shoulder, and strode towards them, his face a picture. 'Why didn't you ring?'

'Because I knew you'd panic.'

'Panic? I don't panic!'

Charlotte started to smile, but then a contraction gripped her and she leant against him, allowing him to hold her up.

'Let's get her in the water,' Bev said decisively, and,

scooping her up in his arms, William carried her down the corridor.

'I can walk,' she told him drily, but he snorted.

'She's supposed to walk around,' Bev reminded him, but he wasn't an obstetrician any more, he was a husband and father.

He helped Bev to undress Charlotte, and then steadied her as she climbed over the side and into the water pool.

'Oh, William, it's wonderful,' she sighed.

There was a tap on the door and the SHO stuck his head round. 'Excuse me, sir—there's a lady in Gynae needs your attention——'

'Tough,' William snapped. 'Get out of here, and get Jake Hunter to come. No one else. OK?'

Charlotte smiled. 'Don't shout at the poor boy.'

Bev slipped out of the door after him, and Charlotte could hear their low-voiced exchange.

A few minutes later Jake came in and crouched beside the pool

'Charlotte? Hi. How's it going?'

'Fine,' she said. It was. She felt almost dreamy, floating in the water, letting her body do what it had been designed for.

'I'm going to see the lady in Gynae for you, but I'll be around—call me if you need me,' Jake said, and with a wink and a grin he left.

Charlotte floated in the warm water, letting the pain of the contractions wash over her, breathing as Bev taught her and as she had learned in antenatal classes.

By midday she was beginning to feel stressed.

She turned to William, who had held her, stroked her, rubbed her back and tummy, murmured words of encouragement and support, never once leaving her side.

'I want you to hold me,' she told him. 'Could you bear to get in?'

'I thought you'd never ask,' he said with a grin. He stripped off his clothes and climbed in beside her, and she felt the slight graze of his hair against her body, the warmth of his chest against her back. She sighed, resting her head on his shoulder.

'Hold me like that—it feels wonderful,' she mumbled, and then another contraction came, worse than all the others.

He soothed her, wiping her face with a cool flannel, pressing iced water to her lips, encouraging and comforting her.

Then everything seemed to stop, and the nature of the contractions changed.

Transition, she realised, and felt the power of her body channelled towards her child. She bowed her head, breathing deeply, and then began to push.

It was like a dream, except for the pain, which she welcomed, because this was one dream she had thought would never come true, and the pain gave it an element of reality.

She heard Bev's voice telling her to pant, and Jake's deeper, gravelly one telling her to hang on, go gently now, just let it happen.

William held her, crouching behind her so that she could push against him, murmuring words of encouragement, and then with one last pant she felt the moment of the baby's birth.

Bev reached down and lifted her baby clear of the water, and as she did so he drew in a great breath and howled in disgust.

'Oh, sweetheart, is it so awful?' she murmured, and, holding him against her breast, she felt the magical touch of his mouth closing over her nipple.

'Oh, God, thank you,' William muttered, and Charlotte turned her head towards him, her joy clearly written on her face.

'Would you like to touch your son?' she asked him, and carefully, reverently, he reached round her and laid his hand on his son's head.

There was a flash, and they looked up to find Jake there, grinning from ear to ear, an instant camera in his hands.

'You owed me that,' he said, and, winking, he turned and left them to it.

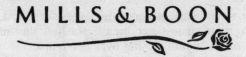

MILLS & BOON

LOVE CALL

The books for enjoyment this month are:

ANYONE CAN DREAM	Caroline Anderson
SECRETS TO KEEP	Josie Metcalfe
UNRULY HEART	Meredith Webber
CASUALTY OF PASSION	Sharon Wirdnam

Treats in store!

Watch next month for the following absorbing stories:

SMOOTH OPERATOR	Christine Adams
RIVALS FOR A SURGEON	Drusilla Douglas
A DAUNTING DIVERSION	Abigail Gordon
AN INDISPENSABLE WOMAN	Margaret Holt

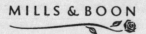

GET 4 BOOKS AND A MYSTERY GIFT

Return the coupon below and we'll send you 4 Love on Call novels absolutely FREE! We'll even pay the postage and packing for you.

We're making you this offer to introduce you to the benefits of Reader Service: FREE home delivery of brand-new Love on Call novels, at least a month before they are available in the shops, FREE gifts and a monthly Newsletter packed with information.

Accepting these FREE books places you under no obligation to buy, you may cancel at any time, even after receiving just your free shipment. Simply complete the coupon below and send it to:

HARLEQUIN MILLS & BOON, **FREEPOST**, PO BOX 70, CROYDON CR9 9EL.

NO STAMP NEEDED

Yes, please send me 4 Love on Call novels and a mystery gift as explained above. Please also reserve a subscription for me. If I decide to subscribe I shall receive 4 superb new titles every month for just £7.20* postage and packing free. I understand that I am under no obligation whatsoever. I may cancel or suspend my subscription at any time simply by writing to you, but the free books and gift will be mine to keep in any case.
I am over 18 years of age.

1EP5D

Ms/Mrs/Miss/Mr _____

Address _____

_____

_____ Postcode _____

mps
MAILING
PREFERENCE
SERVICE

Temptation

Lost Loves

'Right Man...Wrong time'

All women are haunted by a lost love—a disastrous first romance, a brief affair, a marriage that failed.

A second chance with him...could change everything.

Lost Loves, a powerful, sizzling mini-series from Temptation starts in March 1995 with...

The Return of Caine O'Halloran
by JoAnn Ross

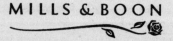

MILLS & BOON